观沧海

中国海洋神话故事

【汉英对照】

陈橙 刘娇 赵雪静－编译

杨帆－绘

CHINESE LEGENDS *of* THE SEAS

中央编译出版社
CCTP Central Compilation & Translation Press

图书在版编目 (CIP) 数据

中国海洋神话故事：汉英对照 / 陈橙，刘娇，赵雪静编译 . -- 北京：中央编译出版社，2019.6
（“观沧海”译丛 / 陈橙主编）
ISBN 978—7—5117—3581—2

I. ①中…
II. ①陈… ②刘… ③赵…
III. 神话 - 作品集 - 中国 - 汉、英
IV. ① I277.5

中国版本图书馆 CIP 数据核字 (2019) 第 090552 号

中国海洋神话故事： 汉英对照

出 版 人：葛海彦
出版统筹：贾宇琰
责任编辑：朱瑞雪
责任印制：刘 慧
出版发行：中央编译出版社
地　　址：北京西城区车公庄大街乙 5 号鸿儒大厦 B 座 (100044)
电　　话：(010) 52612345（总编室） (010) 52612335（编辑室）
(010) 52612316（发行部） (010) 52612346（馆配部）
传　　真：(010) 66515838
经　　销：全国新华书店
印　　刷：北京文昌阁彩色印刷有限责任公司
开　　本：880 毫米 × 1230 毫米 1/32
字　　数：94 千字
印　　张：5.875
版　　次：2019 年 6 月第 1 版
印　　次：2019 年 6 月第 1 次印刷
定　　价：48.00 元

网　　址：www.cctphome.com　　邮　　箱：cctp@cctphome.com
新浪微博：@ 中央编译出版社　　微　　信：中央编译出版社（ID：cctphome）
淘宝店铺：中央编译出版社直销店（http://shop108367160.taobao.com）（010）55626985

目录

第一章

《山海经》始话海洋

Chapter

One

The Classic of Mountains and Seas and the Beginning of Chinese Legends of Seas

上古时候，水神共工怒撞不周山，以致天地崩坏。大地之母女娲为救百姓，炼化五彩石补天，又以巨龟之足充当天柱，撑在天的四角。但是，天地仍然无法恢复平衡，于是地面上的江河都往一处汇流，由此形成了汪洋大海。

随着海的诞生，海上的神明便出现了，东海海神禺虢、南海海神不廷胡余、西海海神弇兹、北海海神禺强在《山海经》中都有所记载。《山海经》中的《海经》部分足足有十三卷，而华夏文明关于海洋的诸多神话就来源于此。《山海经》反映了古代先民对于海洋的认知、探索与向往，体现了强烈的人文精神和鲜明浓郁的海洋文化特色，对中国海洋文化的形成影响深远。据记载，北海海神禺强是一位人面鸟身的神明，他的双耳以青蛇作装饰，脚下踏着两条赤蛇，下面我们要讲的故事就与这位海神有关。

据说，在渤海东边几亿万里的地方，有一个无底的大沟

In ancient times, Gonggong, the God of Water, in anger, knocked his head against Buzhou Mountain, one of the pillars that held up the sky. He broke the pillar in half causing one corner of the earth to collapse. In order to save her people, Nüwa, Mother of the Earth, smelted rocks of five colours and used them to patch up the sky. Then she used the feet of a giant turtle to prop up the four corners of the sky. Yet the universe was unable to restore its balance. Consequently, the rivers converged and transformed into a vast ocean.

After that, the sea gods appeared. *The Classic of Mountains and Seas*[1] portrays Yuguo, the god of the East Sea; Butinghuyu, the god of the South Sea; Yanzi, the god of the West Sea; and Yuqiang, the god of the North Sea. Thirteen of eighteen volumes of *The Classic of Mountains and Seas* are dedicated to the seas (Classic of the Seas) and are the origin of numerous Chinese sea myths. *The Classic of Mountains and Seas* has had a profound influence on Chinese marine culture. It is a reflection of our ancestors' perception of and longing for the ocean. It also embodies a strong humanistic spirit and highlights the distinctive features of marine culture. *The Classic of Mountains and Seas* recounts the story of Yuqiang, a god with the head of a human and the body of a bird, who lived on an island in the middle of the North Sea. He hung two green snakes on his ears and trod two red snakes under his feet.

According to the story of Yuqiang, a bottomless ravine known as Guixu was believed to be lying hundreds of millions of *li*[2] east of Bohai Sea. In this ravine, there were five mountains: Mount Daiyu,

[1]

The Classic of Mountains and Seas or *Shan Hai Jing*, formerly romanized as the *Shan-hai Ching*, is a Chinese classic text and a compilation of mythic geography and myth. It is largely a fabulous geographical and cultural account of pre-Qin China as well as a collection of Chinese mythology. The book is divided into eighteen sections; it describes over 550 mountains and 300 channels.

[2]

1 *li* = 500 meters

壑，名叫归墟。归墟之中有岱舆、员峤、方壶、瀛洲、蓬莱五座仙山。仙山十分雄伟，高度周长都有三万里，甚至山顶的平坦处方圆也有九千里，而山之间的距离足足有七万里。山上住着许多神仙和圣人，他们伴着珍禽异兽，享受着美味珍馐，往返于仙山之间，过得逍遥快活。但是五座山底部并不相连，时常随波浪上下颠簸，不得片刻安稳。山上的神仙和圣人因此十分苦恼，便把此事上报给了天帝。天帝也担心这五座山漂走，神仙和圣人失去居所。

这时天帝想到了海神禺强。因为禺强不但掌管着北海，还主宰着风。他可以化作巨大的鹏鸟，拍一拍翅膀就能激起三千里高的水浪，乘大风盘旋而上可以飞到九万里的高空。既然禺强有着这样的神力，天帝就派禺强指挥十五只巨龟去解决仙山的事情。禺强命巨龟举头托住仙山，避免仙山随波漂流。禺强还安排这十五只巨龟每三只负责一座仙山，分为三班，六万年一轮换，由此，这五座山才稳固下来，山上的神仙和圣人们也不再烦恼。

本以为禺强完满解决了仙山的问题，没想到后来却发生了意外。据说有一个叫龙伯国的地方，那里的人身材十分巨大。有一天，有个龙伯国人十分无聊，抬脚几步便到了仙山所在之地。他垂竿钓起了六只巨龟，并十分高兴地返回了。

Mount Yuanqiao, Mount Fanghu, Mount Yingzhou and Mount Penglai. These majestic mountains were 30,000 *li* each in both height and circumference. The circumference of the plateau at the top (of each mountain) was nearly 9,000 *li* and a distance of up to 70,000 *li* separated one mountain from the other. The mountains were the abode of many immortals and saints who lived a carefree and happy life and also relished the company of good wine, savory dishes, rare birds and beasts. But the mountains were not rooted to the bottom of the sea. As a result, they were very unstable and continuously floated up and down with the waves. The immortals were distressed, so they reported the situation to the Emperor of Heaven. The Emperor of Heaven was worried because the immortals would lose their homes if the five mountains drifted away.

At that moment, the Emperor of Heaven thought of Yuqiang who not only governed the North Sea, but also dominated the wind. He could transform himself into a roc and by flapping his wings, raise waves up to 3,000 *li.* Then riding the wind, he could fly up to a height of 90,000 *li*. Since Yuqiang had such divine powers, the Emperor of Heaven sent him, together with 15 giant turtles, to solve the problem. Under Yuqiang's leadership, the giant turtles bore the fairy mountains with their heads to prevent them from drifting apart. A total of 15 giant turtles were divided into five groups, three for one fairy mountain. Three turtles supported the fairy mountains in turns with each turn lasting 60,000 years. As a result, the mountains became stable, and the fears of the immortals and saints abated.

Unfortunately, their peace of mind did not last long. It is said that there was a country called Longbo close to the mountains.

禺强

Longbo was a country of giants. One day, out of boredom, a giant from Longbo walked a few steps out of his country and ended up in the fairy mountains. He fished out six giant turtles and returned home joyfully. Without the support of the giant turtles, Mount Daiyu and Mount Yuanqiao drifted to the extreme north and gradually sank to the bottom of the sea. The Emperor of Heaven was so infuriated that he punished the whole country. But the damage had been done. At that point, there were only three mountains left: Mount Fanghu, Mount Yingzhou and Mount Penglai.

Although Yuqiang had unimaginable magical powers, he was unable to solve the problem once and for all. The immortals appeared to continue living a leisurely life even though they had deep regrets. As humdrum as the mortals life may have been, they could still create their own legends of the seas. An example is the story Jingwei Determined to Fill up the Sea narrated in *The Classic of Mountains and Seas*.

Nüwa[1] was the youngest daughter of Emperor Yan[2] . She was bright. She was lovely. She was the apple of her father's eye. One day, she was sailing alone in the East Sea. Unfortunately, a storm caused her boat to capsize and she drowned.

But Nüwa did not resign herself to her fate. Her spirit turned into a bird called Jingwei. Jingwei looked like a crow but had a colourful head, a white beak and two red claws. When the bird sang, it sounded like it was yelling its own name.

Jingwei lived on a mountain located in the north. The mountain was covered with cudrana trees. It was called Fajiu Mountain. The bird

[1]

This Nüwa（女娃）is different from Nüwa（女娲）in the beginning of the story. Same PINYIN, but different Chinese characters.

[2]

The Emperor Yan (炎帝) or the Flame Emperor was a legendary ancient Chinese ruler in pre-dynastic times.

少了巨龟支撑的岱舆、员峤两座仙山因此漂流到了极北之地，渐渐沉到海底去了。天帝因此震怒，重重处罚了龙伯国，但事已至此，已无法挽回了。于是，现在就只剩下了方壶、瀛洲、蓬莱三座仙山。

虽然海神禺强有着凡人难以想象的神力，但是仍然没有一劳永逸地解决问题。仙人们看似过得逍遥自在，却也有着无法弥补的遗憾。与之相反，普通生灵虽然没有神力，却也可以写就一段海上传奇，就像《山海经》中所记录的精卫填海的故事。

传说，炎帝有个小女儿，名叫女娃。女娃聪明伶俐，活泼可爱，深得炎帝喜欢。一天，女娃独自驾着小船，到东海去玩耍，不幸的是海上起了风浪，打翻了小船，于是女娃就淹死在东海之中，再也没有回来。

但是女娃并不甘心就这样死去，她的精魂化作了一只小鸟，名叫精卫。这只精卫每每啼鸣都像是在呼喊着自己的名字。精卫鸟体型像乌鸦，但头上长着花纹，同时生着白色的嘴、红色的脚。

精卫鸟住在北方的发鸠山上,山上长满了郁郁葱葱的柘树。她常常飞到西山上去，衔了小树枝或小石子，飞到东海，将树枝或石子投进东海里去。她发誓，一定要把无情的东海填平。

为了实现填平东海的愿望，精卫与海燕结成配偶，并生

would often carry bits of twigs and stones all the way from the West Mountain to the East Sea in a determined effort to fill up the pitiless East Sea.

In order to achieve her goal, Jingwei mated with petrel and gave birth to young birds. The females looked like Jingwei while the males looked like petrel. In spite of the tempestuous sea, Jingwei worked relentlessly day after day because she had her eyes set on her goal. After Jingwei died, her offsprings continued the mission.

What Jingwei had done shocked the gods above. The God of Water, Gonggong, admired Jingwei's perseverance so much that he diverted floodwaters to wash the soil on the plateau into the sea. The East Sea was afraid that one day, it would be filled by Jingwei's offsprings , so, using its tides, it pushed the soil to the shore. The soil was deposited on the shore in the form of a tidal flat. Later, people expanded and transformed the tidal flat into a fertile farmland which nurtured their later generations.

The legend of Jingwei shows the fragility of life and the might of the ocean, but it also praises Jingwei's indomitable spirit of resistance. It encourages people to move towards the ocean in order to explore the unknown. This story has had a dominant influence in China by becoming the source of many poems. Tao Yuanming, a poet of the Eastern Jin Dynasty (AD317 – 420), wrote the following famous lines:

Jingwei, who was drowned in the violent sea,
Carries twigs to fill it by degree.
Xingtian[1], who was beheaded by the god,
Protests by waving his huge shield and rod.

❶

Xingtian: Xingtian vied with the Emperor of Heaven for the leadership. As a result, the Emperor of Heaven beheaded him and buried him on Mount Changyang. Using his nipples as eyes and navel as mouth, Xingtian still wielded his battleaxe and shield, dancing wildly.

下幼鸟。生下的幼鸟中，雌鸟长得像精卫，雄鸟长得则像海燕。精卫鸟早晚不停地从西山衔来石子和树枝，往东海里扔，不畏狂风暴雨，也不惧滔天恶浪。女娃化作的精卫死去之后，还有新的精卫鸟继续来填海。

精卫填海的事震动了天神。水神共工佩服精卫执着的精神，于是就降下洪水，把高原上的泥沙冲进大海。东海害怕自己有一天真的被精卫填平，就把那些泥沙用潮汐推向岸边，泥沙在岸边沉积下来，就形成了滩涂。人们把扩大的滩涂改造成良田，养育了子孙后代。

精卫填海的神话故事展现出了生命的脆弱和海洋的强大，但也赞颂了精卫这种不屈不挠、勇于反抗和斗争的精神，这种精神激励着人们更加勇敢地走向大海，探索未知。精卫填海的故事在中国影响深远，也有很多作家在该题材的基础上创作了大量的诗文。其中最著名的要数东晋诗人陶渊明的诗句："精卫衔微木，将以填沧海。刑天舞干戚，猛志固常在。"此外，精卫填海的故事也被改编或绘制成剧本、电视剧、动画片、歌曲、绘本、油画等形式，一直受到中国人民的喜爱。

除海神禺强和精卫填海的故事外，《山海经》中还记载着大量中国海洋神话故事。作为一本旷古奇书，《山海经》在全世界都有着极大的影响。无论是中国作家鲁迅的叙事散

In addition, the story has been adapted for script,TV dramas, cartoons, songs, picture books, as well as oil paintings. All of these creations have been very popular with the Chinese people.

Besides the story of the Sea God, Yuqiang, and Jingwei, *The Classic of Mountains and Seas* contains a large number of other Chinese sea myths. *The Classic of Mountains and Seas*, which is an extraodinarily special book both in ancient and modern society, has had significant influence all over the world. The profound impact of this book has been demonstrated in a variety of forms including the narrative essay of the Chinese writer Lu Xun, *Ah Chang and The Classic of Mountains and Seas*; the screenplay of the Chinese-French dramatist Gao Xingjian, *The Biography of The Classic of Mountains and Seas*; the recently aired television series *The Classic of Mountains and Seas*; the Japanese *The Pictures of Strange Birds and Animals* in the Edo period; and the field exploration and investigation conducted by the American scholar Dr. Mertz in accordance with the book. This influence stems from people's worship and yearn for the ancient sea gods. The unyielding spirit of the common people who fought against the ocean has been passed down from one generation to another.

We cannot overlook the cultural influence when appreciating stories of sea gods. Thousands of years of agrarian civilization contributed to the shaping of a corresponding concept of space which helped the Chinese civilization to systematically integrate the ocean into a predominantly agrarian lifestyle. Therefore, all of the four sea gods can be traced back to the concept of space espoused in the agrarian culture. Ancient Greece, the origin of western civilization, had a strong relationship with marine culture right from its inception.

文《阿长与〈山海经〉》，还是法籍华裔剧作家高行健的剧本《山海经传》，或者是近几年的电视连续剧《山海经之赤影传说》，更或是日本江户时代的《怪奇鸟兽图卷》，甚至是美国学者墨兹博士按照《山海经》记载而进行的实地探索与考察，无不彰显出《山海经》的巨大影响。这种影响源于人们对拥有神力的远古海神的崇拜和向往，也因人们对普通生灵与海抗争所展现的不屈精神的坚守而得以延续。

在讲述海神的故事时，我们难免要提到文明的传承。中国有着数千年的农耕文明，并由此造就了相应的空间观念，随后我们的文明才逐步由陆地向海洋发展。因此，从某种程度上说，四海海神的定位也源自农耕文明中最原始的空间观念。而西方文明的源头在古希腊，所以它从一开始就是一种海洋文明。这也导致西方文明中的海神与华夏文明中的海神有着较大的差别。在希腊诸神中，海神分为男海神波塞冬和女海神忒提丝，他们并没有职责的明确划分，但各自性格却较为突出。古希腊文明随后发散开去，也就有了古罗马的海神尼普顿，以及两位北欧海神：深海海神埃吉尔和近海海神涅尔德。不同神系中的海神也都留下了很多神话传说，在西方文明中一直流传下来。生活在华夏土地上的人们用自己的方式向世人展现着自己的魂，这正是海的神话的内涵，也是中华文化的精髓。

That is the reason why in western culture, the sea gods are apparently different from those in the Chinese culture. There are two main sea gods in Greek mythology, Poseidon and Thetis. Specifically, they do not have different duties but their characters are disparate. The spread of the Greek culture gave rise to numerous other sea gods such as Neptune of Ancient Rome and Aegir and Njord of Northern Europe. There are countless legends about these sea gods, too. Meanwhile, Chinese people are expected to show their spirit to the world in their own ways —— this is the moral of the sea myths and the essence of Chinese culture.

八方海神佑平安

第二章

Chapter

Two

Sea Gods for Safety and Prosperity

《山海经》中记载了上古时期的四方海神，他们神通广大，却又神秘遥远。因此人们对上古四方海神的信仰，更多地包含着崇拜与敬畏。随着时间的推移，人们的海上探索活动不断扩展和深入，延续下来的海神信仰中也就融入了对平安与富足的向往和期盼。于是出现了许多司掌一事的海神。这些海神各显神通，庇佑百姓平安，留下了诸多精彩的神话故事。

航行保护神

古时候，航海技术有限，出海航行最重要的就是保证平安。但是海上的状况变化莫测，人们常常应对不暇，因此海难频繁发生。为了寻求庇佑，保护航行的海神就出现了，比如晏公神、萧公神，和其他地方性的神灵，如岭南的伏波神。

The Classic of Mountains and Seas portrays four sea gods from ancient times. They were supernatural and mysterious figures worshipped in awe by their subjects. However, as the exploration of the ocean continued, the yearning for safety and prosperity became an integral part of the belief in sea gods. This led to the belief in an array of new-found sea gods. They safeguarded the mariners, and their actions became the source of many fascinating mythic stories.

Sailing Guardians

In ancient times, shipwrecks occurred frequently due to outdated marine technology and unpredictable weather. It was because of this that sailing guardians emerged. They were gods that protected sailors at sea which included Yangong, Xiaogong, and other local gods like Fubo. The following story is about two of these sailing guardians —— Yangong and Fubo.

Yangong had a dark face and bushy eyebrows, and usually wore a red cloak. He was often seen casting spells into the lakes and the seas. One day, a fleet of merchant ships was heading to the market when, suddenly, storm clouds gathered and increasingly became thicker. What quickly followed was the gusting of winds and a torrential downpour. There was a clear possibility the ships would capsize. The terrified merchant threw himself on the deck and

这里我们要讲讲晏公神和伏波神的故事。

据记载，晏公神浓眉虬髯、面如黑漆、身着红袍，常常于江河湖海显灵。相传，有一次，有个商人乘船出海，行至中途，海上天气骤变、阴云密布、狂风大作，数丈高的海浪一会儿将船送上波峰，一会儿又把它卷入浪底。商船颠簸在茫茫大海中，孤立无援、几尽沉没。惊恐万分的商人扑倒在甲板上，虔诚地向晏公神不住祈祷。正在这时，晏公神现身了。惊涛骇浪中，金光乍现，祥云缭绕，一位神人立于浪尖，只见他略施神通，顿时云开日出，风平浪静。商船安稳下来，船上众人无不感念晏公神的庇佑，纷纷拜倒谢恩。晏公神如此这般救人于海难中的事，数不胜数，沿海一带渐渐发展出敬拜晏公神的信仰。人们甚至认为，晏公神不仅能平息风浪，还能赶跑海盗。相传，明嘉靖年间，在倭寇乘夜色偷袭江浙沿海地区时，晏公神搅动风浪，掀翻贼船，溺死倭寇八十余人。

而在岭南地区，信奉伏波神的传统由来已久，其中最有名的一位伏波神就是马援。马援本是东汉光武帝时候的伏波将军，战功卓著，是东汉开国功臣之一。据记载，廉州海中常常有九口巨浪连珠而起，发出雷鸣般的响声，人们无法出海。马援成为伏波神之后，同情受苦的百姓，决意除掉恶浪。浪起时他力挽强弓，箭去如流星，每射一箭就命中一口浪，

piously prayed to Yangong. Yangong heard his prayer and showed up to rescue them. The god man stood on the crest of the waves in the stormy sea as golden lights shone and the clouds dazzled. He calmed the wild wind, dissipated the clouds and quietened the sea. Thereafter, all the ships resumed sailing. Yangong's supernatural powers and his timely intervention marveled the people. Yangong went on to rescue countless people in perilous situations. Along the coast, his popularity soared, the belief in Yangong became firmer and the desire to worship him intensified. People even thought that Yangong could not only calm the wind and waves, but also chase away pirates. During the Jiajing period of the Ming Dynasty (AD1522—1566), when Japanese pirates attempted a surprise attack on China's eastern coastal cities, Yangong created waves which overturned their ships and drowned more than eighty pirates.

The worship of Fubo Gods is a traditional folk belief in China, especially in the Lingnan area. The most famous god is Ma Yuan, officially known as Fubo General (General who calms the waves). Ma Yuan was a politician and general in the Chinese army during the Eastern Han Dynasty (AD25-220). Legend has it that nine huge waves blocked the passage of fishermen to the sea. After he became a Fubo God, Ma Yuan, out of sympathy for the fishermen, used his bow and arrow to shoot down six of the nine wave ssuccessively.However, he had to stop because he ran out of arrows. The Fubo God did not succeed to completely shoot all the waves, but he made it safer for the fishermen to sail. Many temples that were built to dedicate to Ma Yuan still exist nowadays.

大浪随之消失。就这样，马援连射六箭，平息了六口浪。但这时箭没有了，马援只能作罢。因此九口连珠浪就变成了三口，虽然马援没有完全消除连珠浪，但当地百姓的出海航行已经平安了许多。直到今天，还有许多庙宇在供奉着伏波神马援。

风神

“北风航海南风回，远物来输商贾乐。”航海中，海与风是不可分割的，风可以起浪，也可以助航。因此，风神也是一位重要的海神。自古以来，人们信仰的风神也有多位，比如箕伯、飞廉、封姨、屏翳、方天君等。他们产生于不同的时代，也反映不同的地理文化背景。我们将在后面的章节中讲到其中一些风神，这里我们就来讲一讲飞廉的故事。

据说飞廉生得鸟头鹿身，头上长着峥嵘古怪的角，还有一条蛇一样的尾巴。黄帝蚩尤时期，飞廉在祁山修炼。他发现山上有块大石头，每逢风雨来时便飞起如燕，等放晴时，又安伏在原处。飞廉暗暗称奇，便多加留心。一天夜里，这

Wind Gods

"Merchants took advantage of the winds to engage in maritime trade. Eventually, they became prosperous." The sea and the wind are inseparable. The wind can generate waves which can help propel ships. Therefore, the wind god is also an important sea god. In Chinese mythology, there are several gods who control the winds. They include jibo, Feilian, Fengyi, Pingyi and Fangtianjun. These gods belong to different epochs and have different geographical and cultural backgrounds. Some of them are gradually presented in later parts of this narrative. For now, the focus is on the story of Feilian.

According to the legend, Feilian was a strange beast. He had the head of a peacock, the body of a stag and the tail of a snake. He once found a magic stone when he was training in the mountains during the Yellow Emperor time. The stone could float on the tides during the tempest but return to its original position after the storm. Feilian was amazed by this stone and so he kept it very close to himself. One night, the stone transformed into a sack-like monster. It breathed in air and blew it out. Suddenly, a strong gale began gusting and the monster circled over it into the air. Feilian managed to catch the monster at the right moment. Later the monster turned out to be the Mother of Wind who had taught Feilian how to control the wind.

Feilian served under King Zhou[1] from 1075 BC to 1046 BC. After King Wu of Zhou[1] defeated King Zhou, Feilian committed suicide.

[1] King Zhou was the dishonorable and cold-hearted last king of the Shang Dynasty of ancient China.

块大石头动了起来，转眼变成一个形同布囊的无足活物，它吸入空气，然后仰天呼出。顿时，天地间狂风骤起，飞沙走石，活物也随狂风飞旋。飞廉看好时机，一跃而起，抓住了它。原来这活物是风母，飞廉从风母处学会了致风、收风的本事。

到殷纣时期，飞廉为荒淫无道的纣王效力。周武王击败纣王时，飞廉自杀殉国，天帝感动于他的忠诚，赐以石棺葬之，并封他为风神。成为风神之后，飞廉和雨师一起行风布雨，常巡游于海上。在东海之上，若有船只遭遇狂风，飞廉便现身解难。据获救的人说，在吹得人睁不开眼的狂风之中，船上的人隐约看见飞廉像喝水一样把狂风吸入嘴中，他吸完后海风立刻消失，船只也

飞廉

平安脱险。再去看飞廉，他已经像鸟儿一样飞走。讲述飞廉救海难的故事不少，但这些故事大多流传于民间，鲜有文字记载。

潮神

对于依海而生的人们来说，潮水也是很重要的存在，它会带来海产收获，但也会带来灾难。而潮神能够化解潮水带来的灾难，从而获得了人们的信仰。潮神中最有名的当属伍子胥。

伍子胥本是吴王夫差的臣子，因劝谏被赐剑自刎而死。临死前伍子胥嘱托家人将其头颅割下，悬于吴国都城城门之上，这样就可以亲眼看到敌人攻入吴国都城。吴王知道后非常震怒，命人用鸱夷裹盛其尸身，投于长江之中。从此伍子胥在江中因流扬波，依潮往来。江潮怒涨时，人们认为这是伍子胥因愤恨驱水而为之，遂将他奉为潮神。据载，有个叫马亮的人在杭州做知州时，江涛横溢成灾，百姓苦不堪言。马亮曾调兵筑堤，但始终修不成形。马亮没有办法，只好去伍子胥祠献祭祷告。祭祀后的第二天，江潮就退去了，而且江上还出现了横亘数里

The Emperor of Heaven was profoundly moved by Feilian's fidelity, so he buried him in a sarcophagus and conferred him with the status of wind god. Afterwards, Feilian worked in close collaboration with the rain god to nurture all crops and trees. He regularly showed up on the seas to rescue sailors. Whenever a ship was trapped in a squall, Feilian appeared and prevented the disaster from occurring. He sucked fierce winds into his mouth as if he was drinking water. By the time he flew away, Feilian had calmed the wind and quietened the sea. There exist many stories about Feilian's ship rescue missions. However, most of the stories were never written but passed down from generation to generation by word of mouth.

Tidal Gods

The tides have a significant impact on the lives of people who live by the sea. They can bring an abundance of seafood, but at the same time, they can bring disasters. Tidal gods have the ability to prevent these disasters. That is why the unique belief to worship tidal gods developed. The most famous tidal god is Wu Zixu.

During the Warring States era, Wu Zixu was the advisor of Fuchai, the King of Wu. He suggested the king guard against the deceptions of Gou Jian, the King of Yue. Fuchai was infuriated by the advice of Wu Zixu whom he ordered to commit suicide. Wu Zixu's last wish was to have his head hung on the eastern gate where he could witness the destruction of

❶ King Wu of Zhou was the first king of the Zhou dynasty in ancient China.

的沙堤，为修建人工堤坝提供了天然的基础，接下来筑堤工程顺利完工，危害百姓的江潮终于得到遏制。

伍子胥司掌的潮汐并不只限于江河，他也是海上的潮神。《北梦琐言》中记载，五代时，福建某处海域有暗礁威胁船只安全。有一次，闽王梦到吴安王伍子胥托梦，许诺可以帮助他开港导航，于是便派人前往祈祷祭祀。祭祀刚刚结束，海上忽然狂风大作，电闪雷鸣，海中出现数百丈长的庞然大物，怪物奋力跃出海面后又撞击入海。三天后，天空放晴，人们发现海里的暗礁不见了，石港通畅，船只出入变得非常便捷。如今，人们除了为伍子胥立祠供奉之外，还在每年八月潮起时举行祭潮神活动，以感谢伍子胥为庇佑百姓所做的贡献。

船神

海上航行离不开各种船只，古代中国的造船技术曾长时间领先于其他国家，例如郑和下西洋时船队中举世闻名的宝船。中国造船的历史由来已久，船神的信仰也延续了千年，其中有番禺、鲁班、孟公、孟姥、关羽等。这里我们要讲的是船神孟公孟姥的故事。

Wu. Completely enraged by the imprudence of Wu Zixu, the King ordered his corpse to be stuffed in a leather sack and thrown into the river. But the corpse didn't sink into the river. On the contrary, it floated up and down with the waves. That year, there was an unprecedented rise of the tides. The common people believed it was Wu Zixu who worked the tides so they hailed him as the tidal god. History has it that when Ma Liang was serving as the mayor of Hangzhou, there were frequent tidal bores which brought utter misery to the locals. Ma Liang had deployed troops to build a dyke, but it was poorly maintained. Ma Liang had no choice but to pray to Wu Zixu. Just on the very next day, the tidal bore receded. Surprisingly, a sand dyke spanning several miles appeared in the river. They provided a natural foundation for the construction of artificial dikes which were, finally, able to block surging river tides.

Wu Zixu's influence is not limited to the tide of the river, he was also the tidal god of the sea. It was also recorded that during the Five Dynasties and Ten Kingdoms, somewhere in Fujian province the safety of ships was severely threatened by submerged reefs. Min Wang (AD862–925) dreamed that Wu Zixu had promised to help to ease navigation along the ports. As a consequence, he ordered his subordinates to hold a memorial ceremony in honor of Wu Zixu. Towards the very end of the ceremony, a strong wind blew and transformed the hitherto calm waves into rough waves. Then a huge monster appeared. It leaped out of water then went back in several times. Three days later, the weather returned to normal. In addition, the reefs were gone, and the port was unblocked. All these miracles were the work of Wu Zixu, the tidal god. Nowadays, besides worshiping Wu Zixu in the temple, a memorial ceremony is held in appreciation of his benevolence every year in the month of Lunar August.

伍子胥

Ship Gods

Maritime sailing is associated with ships of different varieties. The shipbuilding technology in ancient China was far more advanced than any other countries for a long time. For example, the Chinese Treasure Ship was a large wooden ship in the fleet of Admiral Zheng He, who undertook seven voyages during the early 15th-century Ming Dynasty. China also has a long history of believing in ship gods including Panyu, Lu Ban, Menggong, Mengmu and Guan Yu. The following is the story of the ship gods Menggong and Mengmu.

A long time ago, sailors along the southeastern coastal area kowtowed to the ship gods and called their names several times prior to setting sail. This was a

在东南沿海一带，行船前要三拜三呼船神的名字，以除百忌。有些地方在夜间行船前要杀鸡，用鸡骨占卜吉凶，用鸡肉进行祭祀，同时呼唤孟公孟姥的名字，祈求一路顺风。船家求祷的孟公孟姥，就是沿海地区人们信奉的船神。据说，古时候有一艘大船在狂风暴雨中遇险，船上的人苦苦支撑。就在大家筋疲力尽的时候，突然发现前方茫茫的黑暗中出现了火光。众人用尽全力操纵船只向前驶去。靠近后发现，原来是一位和善的老汉手提灯火，等在一座小岛的岸边。老汉带领众人来到自家茅屋。屋里一位慈祥的老妇人早已熬好粥食，分盛给大家。众人吃完后，倦意袭来，纷纷睡去。等再醒来时，发现自己竟然在船上，而船只早已脱离风暴，临近家乡的海岸了。后来人们再去找寻那座小岛和老夫妇时，已无迹可循。人们想到，这一定是临行前祭祀的孟公孟姥在庇佑着他们。这样的故事，口口相传，越传越广，渔民海商们纷纷宰杀三牲，敬奉孟公孟姥，以求庇护。

海产诸神

对于生活在海边的百姓来说，除了希望不受海潮海风侵

ritual intended to ensure a safe voyage. In some areas, people sacrificed chickens and then used the bones from the sacrificed chickens to tell the future. At the same time, sailors prayed to Menggong and Mengmu, the ship gods, for a successful voyage. It is said that at one point, a ship was caught in a storm at sea and was on the verge of capsizing. The sailors had all given up hope but at that critical moment, a bright light appeared on the horizon. They did everything they could to move towards it. Then they found an old man on the shore of an island. He was holding a lantern. The old man took the sailors to a thatched cottage. In the cottage was an old woman who had already cooked some porridge for the sailors. After eating the porridge, the sailors drifted off to sleep. When they woke up, they found themselves on their ship. They also realized that the storm was raging far behind them and they were approaching the coast. Later, the sailors tried in vain to locate the island and the old couple. They believed that it must have been Menggong and Mengmu who had helped them. The locals passed down the story by word of mouth. In addition, all fishermen and merchants prayed to Menggong and Mengmu by sacrificing livestock.

Marine Gods

Besides wishing to be free from rough tides and gusting sea winds, the people living by the sea longed to have abundant seafood which they considered fundamental to a peaceful life. Some marine gods are responsible for seafood. As a result, they are worshipped in

袭、航行平安外，更期望的是获得丰硕的海产，有了收获才能安身立命，丰衣足食。有一些海神，司掌海产，人们敬奉这些海神以期望获得好的收成。这些海神包括盐神夙沙氏、鱼神杨甫老大、长年公、楚太、陈乌梅等。这里，我们讲讲鱼神陈乌梅的故事。

相传，陈乌梅原本是一个穷苦渔民。一次出海时，他救了一条搁浅在礁石上的大鱼，大鱼为报答他的救命之恩，告诉他说："你用我的眼泪擦眼睛，就能透过海水看到鱼群。"陈乌梅听了大鱼的话，用鱼泪擦眼，果然以后每次出海捕鱼都能满载而归。渔行老板知道后，派人重金收买陈乌梅为自己捕鱼，但是被陈乌梅拒绝了。于是歹毒的渔行老板暗中派人挖掉了陈乌梅的眼睛，不让他再继续捕鱼。但是陈乌梅仍坚持上船，帮助其他渔民。他用耳朵仍能听到鱼群的声音，经他的指点，渔民仍然能捕到很多鱼。于是，渔行老板干脆派人杀了陈乌梅，把尸体扔到荒僻的小岛。渔民们找到他的尸体，葬在岛的最高处，面向东方，修建了庙宇，并尊他为"鱼神爷"。渔民们还在船头画上一双眼睛，表示纪念。后来，陈乌梅托梦给渔民，叫他们把船底刷成白色，这种白底船一出海，鱼群就游来，渔民因此而受益。庙宇中的鱼神像，一副渔民打扮，紫铜色脸膛，穿赭衣笼裤，左手擎黄鱼，右

anticipation for the best possible harvest. These gods include the Salt God, Su Shashi and the fish gods, Yangfu Laoda, Changniangong, Chutai and Chen Wumei. The narrative that follows is about Chen Wumei, a fish god.

Originally, Chen Wumei was a poor fisherman. One day he accidentally saved a big fish that was stranded on a rock. In order to return the favor, the fish shed tears and then said to Chen, "If you wipe your eyes with my tears, you will see shoals of fish through sea water." Chen did exactly what the fish had told him. After that, each time he went fishing, he returned with a lot of fish. After learning about this story, a fish merchant offered Chen Wumei a large sum of money to hire him. When Chen refused the offer, the merchant secretly sent someone to gouge out his eyes. In spite of his blindness, Chen continued to assist other fishermen to catch fish with his acute sense of hearing. Exasperated, the merchant killed Chen and dumped his corpse on to a desolate island. But some fishermen found his body, buried him on the top of the island and built a temple for him facing the east. Fishermen then honored Chen Wumei with the title "Fish God" and, to remember him, they painted eyes on the prows of their boats. Later, Chen appeared in a fisherman's dream and instructed him to tell every fisherman to paint the bottom of their ship white. As soon as the ships sailed out of the bay, scores of fish gathered around them. Every fisherman benefited from this practice. The statue of the Fish God in the temple is dressed as a fisherman. He has a bronzed face, a reddish-brown shirt, and loose pants. On his left hand is a fish and, on his right, a fish spear. Whenever the tide came, fishermen prayed to him for a good catch.

Whether it is sailing guardians, wind gods, tidal gods, ship gods or

手举鱼叉。每逢海汛，渔民都要前去祭拜，祈求丰收。

无论是航行保护神，还是风神、潮神、船神和海产诸神，都在各自司掌的领域庇佑着靠海为生的普通百姓，正所谓八方海神佑平安。海神们也因为庇佑百姓平安而获得了人们虔诚的敬拜和庄重的尊崇。从上古四方海神到后来的诸海神，信仰的传承和发展表明，人类从远古走来，已从对海洋的单纯敬畏，转变为对海洋的向往和探索，正是人们一往无前地探索海洋的勇气，和不知疲倦地开拓未知领域的进取精神，成为人类续写海洋文明的不竭动力。

marine gods, all of them are fulfilling their duties to protect the people living by the sea. That's why there is such a strong belief in the sea gods. In light of the continuation and development of faith in the gods, it is clearly perceptible that the awe for the sea morphed into a yearning to explore it. It is the indomitable courage of people to discover the ocean and the relentless pioneering spirit to explore the unknown that has transformed into the insatiable quest for humans to advance marine culture.

In ancient China, the capital was usually built in the Central Plains or the North, the southeastern seas were therefore called the South China Sea.

南海观音度众生

第三章

Chapter

Three

Guanyin of the South China Sea Giving Relief and Help to All Beings

佛家以慈悲为怀，常常讲到“大慈与一切众生乐，大悲拔一切众生苦”。在佛家诸神中，有一位菩萨寻声救苦、度化众生，她就是观世音菩萨。佛家把世界分为东胜神洲、南瞻部洲、西牛贺洲、北俱芦洲，中国属于南瞻部洲。南瞻部洲有一座山，名叫普陀山，是观世音菩萨的道场。中国古代，大多建都中原或者北方，东南海域就被称为南海，而普陀山位于南海之中，因此观世音菩萨又被称为南海观音。

自古以来，南海观音就广为人们信奉。这不只是因为她是佛教西方三圣之一，更重要的是她常常向处于苦难中的人们伸出援手。东晋时，僧侣法显去西方求经，归来之时乘船渡过东海，遇上了大风，船在风浪的侵袭下破损漏水。船上的商人开始丢掉货物以减轻载重，法显害怕船商把佛像经文丢掉，就匆忙把所带的衣服、食物和杂物扔到海中，然后诚心向观音求祷：“我远行求法，愿神威归流，得到所止。”

Buddhism promotes leniency toward all beings. Buddha provides love and makes life easy and peaceful for all beings. Out of compassion, he equally lifts the suffering of beings. The Buddhist goddess, Avalokitesvara, known in Chinese as Guanyin, rids people of their suffering while offering salvation to sentient beings. Guanyin is the short form of Guanshiyin which means, "The One Who Perceives the Sounds of the World," or "Goddess of Mercy." In Buddhism, the world was divided into four continents: Purvavideha[1], Jambudvipa [2],Aparagodaniya[3], and Uttarakuru[4]. China is part of Jambudvipa.In ancient China, the capital was usually built in the Central Plains or the North, the southeastern seas were therefore called the South China Sea. It is claimed that Mount Putuo, located in the South China Sea, is the academy of Guanyin. Because of this, Guanyin is also known as Guanyin of the South China Sea.

In Buddhism, Guanyin is widely worshipped not only because she is one of the "Three Saints of the West."Rather, she is worshipped mostly because of her willingness to lend a hand to sufferers. During the Eastern Jin Dynasty (AD317–420), a monk named Faxian went to the West in search of Buddhist scriptures. On his way back, he had to

[1] Purvavideha: one of the four continents situated to the East of Mount Meru. It is semi-circular in shape, white in color and flanked by the two subcontinents Deha and Videha.

[2] Jambudvipa: one of the four continents situated to the South of Mount Meru. Its shape is trapezoidal. It is the human world in which we live.

[3] Aparagodaniya: one of the four continents situated to the West of Mount Meru. It is shaped like a circle with a circumference of about 7,500 yojanas (Sarvastivada tradition).

[4] Uttarakuru: one of the four continents situated to the North of Mount Meru.

大风昼夜不停地刮了十三天，但法显乘坐的船却奇迹般地被吹到一座小岛边而得救。接下来的路上，一天夜里他们又遇到暴风雨，黑暗中船上的商人和乘客惊恐万分，法显“一心念观世音……”观音菩萨仿佛听到了他的祷告，商船安然捱过黑夜，迎来了破晓，一行人再次化险为夷。法显求经路上，经历了许多艰险，但他总能死里逃生，转危为安。法显认为这都是蒙神佛保佑，正如《佛国记》所云：“……（法显）是以不顾微命，浮海而还，艰难具更，幸蒙三尊威灵，危而得济……”

观音菩萨在海难中显灵救人的故事还有很多。天竺译师求那跋陀罗来华时，乘船行至中途，海风停住，船只不能扬帆，无法前行，而船上淡水却逐渐消耗，一船人忧心忡忡。跋陀就对众人说：“可同心并力念十方佛，称观世音，何往不感。”然后开始密诵咒经，恳到礼忏。随即天气骤变，狂风大起，乌云铺满天空，大雨倾盆而至，一船人的危难顿时化解。大家都知道是观世音施手救助，回到岸上之后，纷纷劝人信奉观音，成了观音的传布者。

南海观音救人于海难之中，像海神一样庇佑着人们，也展现了佛家如海洋般博大深邃的慈悲胸怀。因此在东南沿海一带，人们往往信奉南海观音。即便有人家不信奉佛教，也

cross the East China Sea by ship. Unfortunately, his ship was severely damaged because it was caught in a violent sea storm. Faxian was afraid that the captain would attempt to save the ship by discarding the statues and scriptures of Buddha, so he threw all his clothes, food and clutter overboard. Then he offered the following prayer to Guanyin, "I travelled a long distance to obtain these Buddhist scriptures, I hope that I can bring back these precious materials to promote Buddhism. Please help me." Though, for thirteen days the storm raged on, the ship miraculously drifted to an island and people on board were saved. Later during the journey, the ship once again encountered a storm and once again, Faxian prayed to Guanyin who helped them to successfully weather the storm. Faxian had to overcome tremendous obstacles on his voyage in quest for the Sutras but was able, on each occasion, to turn the corner. As the Book of the Buddhas puts it: "... in total disregard of his personal safety, Faxian traveled across the sea with the blessings of Guanyin and Buddha..."

This is not the only story that recounts how Guanyin rescued people in need. Gunabhadra (394–468), an Indian Mahayana Buddhist monk , travelled to China for a visit. Unfortunately, his ship lacked wind power and was unable to advance. This led to an acute shortage of fresh water for the crew. People on the ship became extremely worried. Gunabhadra told the crowd to pray fervently to Guanyin and they did. Immediately, the weather changed. Dark clouds amassed, and rain poured resolving the crisis. People understood that it was the work of Guanyin. When they arrived at the shore, they became apostles of Guanyin and urged everyone to worship her.

Guanyin protected people just like sea gods did, and her actions

观音

depicted the leniency and philanthropy of Buddhism. Therefore, in the southeastern coastal areas, most people believe in Guanyin. Those who do not believe in Buddhism also show a tremendous amount of reverence for her. As one of the Three Saints of the West, Guanyin had supernatural powers and subdued many monsters that troubled the locals.

Zhoushan is located in Zhejiang province. The name Zhoushan originated from a story in which Guanyin subdued the King of the Sea. A monster who called himself King of the Sea lived in East China Sea near Mount Putuo. The ferocious creature forcibly occupied Penglai Island out of sheer greed. Guanyin knew about this forced occupation, so she transformed into a fisherwoman. Using her magical powers, she confronted Admiral Sha, a subordinate of King of the Sea, who had been ordered to splash water all over the Penglai Island using his gold lacquer footbath. The water became a flood that nearly inundated the Island. The flood was also about to reach the locals but they were saved after Guanyin casting a spell, which

对南海观音怀有崇敬之心。身为西方三圣之一，南海观音有着无上法力,不仅能平息海难,还降伏了许多为害一方的精怪。

今天，浙江有一个叫作舟山的地方，而“舟山”这个名字就来自观音降伏海大王的故事。在普陀山东边的大海里，有一个叫作海大王的妖怪，霸占了蓬莱岛，残暴地欺压附近的百姓。观音知道后化为渔妇，和海大王手下的傻将军斗法。海大王命傻将军使用法宝金漆脚盆，谁知傻将军一盆水泼下去淹了蓬莱。眼看大水就要祸及周边百姓，观音立即施法将金漆脚盆变作一条大帆船，救起了百姓，并让他们在普陀山附近住下，从此这里就被称作舟山。

据《观音得道》一书记载，海里有一种鳌鱼，长得似鱼非鱼，似龟非龟，头生得和龙头相似，但没有须，身披重重的厚甲，也有四只脚。它平时居于水底，觅食时浮出水面，虽身体硕大，却行动极快，甚至能上岸爬行，吞吃猪羊，而且特别喜欢吃人。沿海居民深受其害，苦不堪言。观音菩萨得知后，用十万八千根蚕丝结成一个羂索，又取宝瓶中的杨柳削成有九个倒刺的鱼钩，系在羂索的一端。然后，再用沙土做成一个泥人，将鱼钩藏在泥人腹内做成鱼饵。鳌鱼一露面，观音就将鱼饵抛出。那鳌鱼不明就里，一口吞下泥人。泥人一入鳌腹，立刻化掉，那有九个倒刺的鱼钩便锁住鳌鱼

turned the gold lacquer footbath into a huge ship. Later, Guanyin arranged for the locals to live near Mount Putuo and from then on, the place became known as Zhoushan (In Chinese, Zhou means ship, Shan means mountain).

In addition, historical records suggest that there existed a turtle that closely resembled a fish. The turtle had the head of a dragon but without the antenna. It lived at the bottom of the water and only emerged to forage. Despite its enormous size, it moved very fast. It could even crawl ashore to eat pigs and sheep. In particular, it liked to eat people. Coastal residents were incapable of killing it. They simply suffered from the turtle's atrocious activities. After Guanyin learned about their situation, she used 108,000 pieces of silk to form a rope. She also made nine barbed hooks with wickers in her bottle,which she fastened at one end of the rope. After that, she made a clay figurine out of sand and hid the hooks in its belly. The turtle mistook the clay figurine for a human, and immediately opened its mouth and swallowed it. The clay figurine began to melt away in its stomach, and the barbed hooks punctured the turtle's heart causing it to writhe in agony. At this point, Guanyin said, "You have lived in the world for so long and have done considerable harm to many creatures. I would have killed you right away, but I give you the chance to come with me to the South China Sea to practice Buddhism. Do you want to come or not?" The turtle nodded eagerly. Therefore, Guanyin jumped on the back of the turtle and together they went to the South China Sea.

Because of the popularity of tales describing how she tamed the turtle and saved the populace, portraits of Guanyin, till date, have her standing on the turtle's back and holding a fish basket. Folks also

的心脏，疼得它在沙滩上直打滚。观音菩萨这时现身，说道："孽畜，你在人间许久，残害诸多生灵，理当诛灭，我本慈悲之旨度你到南海修行，忏除夙孽，你愿也不愿？"言毕，化去绳钩，鳌鱼听了点头归顺。于是观音踏上鳌背，乘浪而去。

观音降鳌鱼、救百姓的故事广为流传，因此就有了手提鱼篮、脚踏鳌鱼、神态威严的鱼篮观音形象。民间认为鱼篮观音法力无边，相关的故事也有很多，人们熟知的《西游记》中就有记载。除了降妖除魔，观音菩萨甚至还为一方神仙化解危难。在《观音修道香山记》中就有这样一个故事。

一天，观音正在打坐诵经，忽然从窗外投进一缕奇异的霞光。观音于霞光中见到一处闹市。闹市里有一位老渔翁正在叫卖鲜鱼，鱼篓中有一条金翅金鳞的大鲤鱼，格外惹眼。再细看，金色鲤鱼眼含哀痛，隐有泪水，似乎在苦苦哀求。观音掐指一算，知道了这金色鲤鱼正是南海龙王的三太子。原来，那日三太子奉命巡海，但他不听劝谏，化作一条金色大鲤鱼，在海水中巡游。谁知他刚出游不久，就遇到一艘小渔船。船上的老渔翁一网撒下，不偏不倚正好将龙三太子收入网中。龙王正在龙宫召群臣议事，得知太子遭难，立刻发兵救援。等救兵赶去，老渔翁早已收网回岸，龙王也奈何不得了。龙王立刻向观音求助，哭诉道："如若这条鱼被市井

regard Fish-Basket Guanyin as a symbol of infinite power. Many tales related to Fish-Basket Guanyin have been recorded in many books including Journey to The West. The goddess with infinite power could not only eliminate evil but also help gods to resolve crises. The tale that follows describes how Guanyin saved the young dragon prince of the Southern Dragon King.

One day, Guanyin was meditating when a ray of sunlight shone through the window. She saw a bustling market in the ray. There was an old fisherman selling fresh fish but the most eye-catching image was that of a golden carp. After examining closely, she noticed that there were tears in its eyes and it seemed to be pleading. It turned out to be the third son of the Southern Dragon King. The young thrill-seeking dragon prince had ventured out of the dragon palace, transformed into a golden carp and had gone swimming in the ocean. Unfortunately, he was netted by a fisherman and was later sold to a fishmonger. When the Dragon King learned about what had happened, he was in panic. He prayed to Guanyin to save his son. This was because on land, he had no powers. His piteous cries reached Guanyin who immediately dispatched one of her dharmapalases with gold to purchase the fish before the villagers did. Unfortunately, when the young man reached the market, the fish had already been purchased by a villager. So, the young man paid a high price to get it back from the villager.

He brought back the fish in a bamboo basket and set it free into the ocean. But that was not the end of the story. To reward Guanyin for her help, the Southern Dragon King sent his daughter, a girl called Long Nü ("dragon girl") to present Guanyin with "Pearl of Light," a precious jewel owned by the Dragon King which shone day and night.

小民买去烹食，则吾儿小命休矣。唯望观音菩萨施手相救，大恩龙宫永世不忘。”观音菩萨旋即命护法神韦驮化作一个凡人去救龙三太子。韦驮赶到闹市，发现金鲤早已被人买走，韦驮赶紧找到买主，重金买下金色鲤鱼，这才救下龙三太子。

韦驮将鲤鱼放在竹篮里带到海边，并最终放归大海。但故事并未就此结束。为报观音大恩，龙王派龙女向观音呈献了夜明珠。而龙女在见到观音后，为观音所折服，请求拜观音为师，侍奉左右，观音菩萨答应了她的请求。这就是我们经常看到的鱼篮观音手持夜明珠画的缘起。

南海观音救凡人于危难之际，降服为害一方的精怪，还救了龙三太子性命，保龙族血脉，称得上是真正意义的普度众生。这些故事只是无数世代流传的民间传说的一部分。实际上，在中国数千年的历史中，观音的影响遍及方方面面。

首先，观音信仰是中华民族传统文化的重要组成部分。观音除了在中原地区广被信奉，藏族、白族、契丹等少数民族也供奉观音。尤其是在藏族地区，观音菩萨被称为“雪域怙主”，是藏族人民的造物神和守护者。据记载，伦赞王妃就是因为受到观音菩萨感召才诞下松赞干布王子。

其次，观音菩萨还与其他神灵有着紧密联系。比如妈祖的出生就与观音有关。传说妈祖的母亲向观音祈祷生下了妈

Long Nü, overwhelmed by the presence of Guanyin, asked to be her disciple so that she might study the Buddha Dharma. Guanyin accepted her request. That explains why we always find paintings of Guanyin carrying a bamboo basket with a single fish and holding a large pearl.

Guanyin demonstrated her prowess and benevolence by saving ordinary people, subduing formidable monsters and helping dragons. That is her way of offering relief and help to all beings. But these accounts only form a tiny portion of the stories and legends we know today. As a matter of fact, Guanyin has influenced almost every aspect of our lives during thousands of years of Chinese history.

First and foremost, the belief in Guanyin is a fundamental part of the culture and tradition of the Chinese nation. The belief has been propagated among the Han people as well as other ethnic minorities. The worship of Guanyin is deeply rooted among Tibetans, Khitans and the Bai people. In the Tibetan areas, Guanyin, called the "goddess of snowland, "is the creator and protector of Tibetans. It is said that it was under the inspiration of Guanyin that Driza Tökarma gave birth to Songtsen Gampo [1].

Moreover, Guanyin is closely related to many other gods. For example, Mazu was born because her mother had prayed to Guanyin. Mazu became increasingly powerful when she was growing up because she learned from the Avalokitasvara Sūtra.

Lastly, Guanyin has a wide range of duties. She is the candlelight of the weak, the protector of women and children, and she helps people escape from immense sufferings. The goddess pays special attention to the helpless, especially children and women. Guanyin is also known as "Child-Sending Guanyin." That means, women longing to have a child

[1] Songtsen Gampo: the 33rd Tibetan king and founder of the Tibetan Empire, and is traditionally credited with the introduction of Buddhism to Tibet.

祖，妈祖从小诵经礼佛不辍，五岁就能诵读《观音经》，后来渐渐灵通变化，终成护佑一方的海神。

最后，观音菩萨还承担了多重神圣的职能。她帮助百姓消灾解厄，保佑人们风调雨顺，大慈大悲，救苦救难。甚至还掌管生育，保护妇孺，比如送子观音。民间习俗认为，诵《观音经》、瞻观音像、向观音祈求，都是得子契机。在《南海慈航》中就有“梦白衣大士笑容可拥，抱一孩子置踏，次日生子，岁余如前梦，又生一子”的记载。由此可见，南海观音以慈悲之心救众生，其信仰也长盛不衰。

观音菩萨是古印度佛教中，西方极乐世界阿弥陀佛的弟子，和大势至菩萨伴随阿弥陀佛左右，合称西方三圣。佛教传入中国后，观音在汉传佛教中的信仰极为广泛，并在中国民间形成了不同于古印度的观音信仰。在中国民间的观音信仰形态中，观音菩萨掌管多重职能，如同多位神祇的集合。在西方文明的神系中，如古埃及、古希腊和北欧众神中，并没有与观音菩萨旗鼓相当的神灵，例如在希腊众神中，掌管婚姻、生育，保护妇女的神灵是赫拉，智慧、农业、航海之神是雅典娜，医药、消灾解难之神是阿波罗，三位神灵所担负的职责之和才大致与观音菩萨相当。这也进一步说明观音菩萨在汉传佛教和中国民间信仰体系中影响巨大，在中国传

may read the Avalokitasvara Sūtra and pay their respect to Guanyin to increase their chances of having a baby. According to another account, "A smiling immortal who was holding a child visited a woman in her dream. The following day, she gave birth. A year later, the woman had the same dream, and again, she gave birth to her second child." The belief in Guanyin has continued to gain momentum because of her compassion.

According to ancient Indian Buddhism, Guanyin Bodhisattva is a disciple of Amitabha. Amitabha, Guanyin, and Bodhisattva of Great Power are called the "Three Saints of the West." Since the introduction of Indian Buddhism in China, the belief in Guanyin has spread widely but it also took on a different form. In Chinese folk belief, Guanyin has multiple responsibilities. She appears to play the role of many gods putting together. Among ancient Egyptian, Greek, and Nordic gods, there was none comparable to Guanyin. For example, Hera, in ancient Greek mythology, was the goddess of marriage, childbirth and women while Athena was the ancient Greek goddess of wisdom, agriculture and navigation. On his part, Apollo was the god of medicine, healing, and plague. The responsibilities of the three gods are roughly equivalent to those of Guanyin. This further illustrates the great influence that Guanyin Bodhisattva has on Chinese Buddhism and the Chinese folk belief system, and the far-reaching role of Guanyin in various aspects of Chinese traditional society.

In today's modern society, the belief in Guanyin has endured as it has continued to spread. An endless stream of pilgrims continues to visit numerous Guanyin temples to pay tribute to her. Believers burn incense, pray, read Avalokitasvara Sūtra, build Guanyin statues

统社会的方方面面发挥着广泛作用。

在现代社会中，观音信仰仍然历久弥坚，长盛不衰。无数的寺庙中观音殿香火旺盛，善男信女们虔诚地发愿还愿、诵观音经、塑观音像、吃斋念佛。影视剧中也常常出现观音的形象，比如《西游记》《白蛇传》《妈祖》等电视剧中，观音菩萨总是解危救难，降妖除魔。对观音的信仰代表着人们对真善美的追求，对幸福生活的美好向往。

and abstain from eating meat all in the effort to express their piety to Guanyin. In movies and TV series including Journey to The West, The Tale of The White Snake and Mazu, Guanyin often delivers all beings from torment and helps the needy. The belief in Guanyin acts as a spiritual guide for people to pursue a better life as well as truth, goodness and beauty.

四海龙王遨天地

第四章

Chapter

Four

The Legends of the Dragon Kings of Four Seas

随着四海观的形成，开始出现了掌管四海的神灵，如第一章所讲《山海经》中记载的四海海神。龙的形象在华夏文明初期就已形成，在儒释道三家的影响下，四海龙王直至宋朝才正式成为一种海神信仰，并于明清达到极盛。有关四海龙王的记载繁杂各异，这里选取流传最广的一种，即东海龙王敖广、西海龙王敖闰、南海龙王敖钦、北海龙王敖顺。下面我们就先说西海龙王敖闰的故事。

相传很久以前四海龙王还是四位龙子。随着时间的流逝，四位龙子都已长大，却整日无所事事。于是，这四兄弟每天翻江倒海，搅得龙宫不得安宁。龙子们的父亲不堪其扰，终于想到一个办法。他召来四位龙子，命大儿子敖广做东海龙王，二儿子敖钦做南海龙王，三儿子敖顺做北海龙王。他本想留下小儿子敖闰在身边，可小儿子执意要去做西海龙王，老龙王没办法只好答应。敖闰独自往西而去，可他找遍九州，

When the idea of the Four Seas was initially perceived, four gods, like the gods in *The Classic of Mountains and Seas*, appeared to take charge of the four seas. Although the image of the dragon had been conceived right from the beginning of the Chinese civilization, it was not until the Song Dynasty (AD960–1279) that the current form of the Dragon Kings of the Four Seas, shaped under the influence of Confucianism, Buddhism and Taoism, gradually took shape. The popularity of the Dragon Kings increased significantly during the Ming and Qing dynasties (AD1368–1911). A lot of stories about the Dragon Kings of Four Seas have been documented in Chinese history. Here we focus on the most popular versions of the stories about Ao Guang, the Dragon King of the East Sea; Ao Shun, the Dragon King of the North Sea; Ao Qin, the Dragon King of the South Sea; and Ao Run, the Dragon King of the West Sea whose story begins our narrative accounts.

When the Dragon Kings of Four Seas were still four dragon princes, they hung out all day and regularly brewed storms on rivers and seas, causing huge currents in the Dragon Palace. Because their father was so annoyed, that he came up with an idea to solve this problem. He assembled his sons one day and ordered the eldest son, Ao Guang, to become the Dragon King of the East Sea. Similarly, he made his second son, Ao Qin, the Dragon King of the South Sea while his third son, Ao Shun, was ordered to become the Dragon King of the North Sea. He wanted to keep his youngest son, Ao Run, around, but the young prince insisted on becoming the Dragon King of the West Sea. He had no choice but to agree. When Ao Run sailed westwards alone, he looked around but could not find the West Sea anywhere. When he arrived at Qilian Mountain, Ao Run couldn't help weeping

也未发现西海。最后他来到祁连山麓，精疲力竭地停下来。敖闰又累又失望，忍不住伤心哭泣。哭毕，他决定自己造出西海。于是，他登上祁连山顶，筑坛施法，霎时间狂风大作，却仅落下几滴雨水。敖闰施法多日未见成效，却惊动了玉皇大帝。玉帝感念他的诚心，便令雷公、电母、风伯、云童相助。顷刻间电闪雷鸣，狂风大作，暴雨骤落。数日之后，一片碧波万顷，深不见底的汪洋现于敖闰面前，这便是西海。自此以后，敖闰就在这里做起了西海龙王。

不知又过了多少年，西海周围大旱，草木皆枯，牲畜饥渴，人们已无法度日。西海龙王同情百姓，决定施法救助。他变回龙身，腾空而起，张口吸掉大半海水，然后龙口一喷，顿时天降大雨，千里草原得救。然而西海从此却变成了一个小湖，也就是现在的博斯腾湖。人们感念西海龙王敖闰的救命之恩，便在通天河的河口岛上为他修建了一座庙，庙里供着他的全身塑像。人们朝夕前往敬香，香火长盛不衰。

有关四海龙王的记载中，现存最多的要数东海龙王。《酉阳杂俎》中就记载了这样一则故事。唐武则天时期，有一位书生随新罗使者一起出海。途中一阵大风吹来，书生被卷到一个奇怪的地方。那里人人长着长须，却讲着中国话，书生与之攀谈，方知到了“长须国”。后来长须国国王封书生做

since he was both exhausted and dejected. He wiped his tears in a determined effort to create the sea himself. So Ao Run climbed to the top of Qilian Mountain and cast a spell. Suddenly, a heavy gale-force wind developed but brought only a few drops of rain. He steadfastly cast magical powers for several days to no avail. The Jade Emperor heard his struggle and ordered the God of Thunder, the God of Lightning, the God of Wind and the God of Cloud to help this young prince. Almost immediately, there was thunder and lightning followed by a torrential downpour. After several days, Ao Run could relish the sight of an endless and bottomless ocean. That was the West Sea. Since then, Ao Run was recognized as the Dragon King of the West Sea.

Some years later, the area near the West Sea was hit by a severe drought. Trees and grass withered animals starved, and people were dehydrated to the point where no one could guarantee they would see the light of the following day. The Dragon King of the West Sea became sympathetic to the plight of the locals so he made up his mind to help them. As he leapt into the air, Ao Run transformed himself into a dragon, opened his large mouth, sucked away half of the water in the West Sea and spurted it out. What followed was a heavy downpour that rejuvenated the boundless grassland. After that, the West Sea became a small lake called Bosten Lake[1]. In appreciation to the Dragon King, the locals built a temple on an island and enshrined the image of the Dragon King in it. Thereafter, an endless stream of pilgrims went to the temple to offer incense.

Of the legends that were recorded about the Dragon Kings of the Four Seas, the stories of the Dragon King of the East Sea were the most dominant. One of such stories is found in *The Miscellaneous Morsels*

[1] Bosten Lake is a freshwater lake on the northeastern rim of the Tarim Basin, about 20km east of Yanqi and 57km northeast of Korla, Xinjiang, China.Located in the Bayin'gholin Mongol Autonomous Prefecture.

了司风长，并把公主许配于他。书生尽享荣华富贵，日子过得十分惬意。有一天，长须国君臣上下皆满面愁容，书生便去问个究竟。那国王哭着说：“我国将有大难，还请驸马去谒见东海龙王，只说东海第三汊第七岛长须国，有难求救即可。我国太过偏远，请你务必反复求情。”说罢，国王派人以船相送。书生登上船，不过瞬息之间便到了东海。

书生来到龙宫，说明自己是长须国使者，龙王亲自相迎。书生说明来意，龙王即命查明情况。过了许久，属下报告说：“东海之内并无此国。”书生想起长须国国王的嘱托，又再次恳求，并申明长须国在东海第三汊第七岛。龙王只好令属下再次细细查寻。过了一顿饭的工夫，那人再次来报，说：“长须国是个虾岛，此月应该供应大王食料。”东海龙王一听，哈哈大笑：“原来如此！我虽为东海之王，但每月食料都由天庭安排，不胡乱捕食。既然你为它们求情，那我就网开一面，减少这个月的食料吧。”于是命属下将长须国虾王等放归海中，又派使者送书生回家。一夜之间，船就行至山东登州。书生上岸，使者与船便都消失不见，一切仿佛梦境一般。

西海龙王倾一海之力救旱灾中的百姓，东海龙王网开一面赦长须国之灾，而南海龙王也有着自己的故事。明清时，

from Youyang.

During the reign of Wu Zetian [1], a young scholar embarked on a sea voyage with an envoy from Silla. They encountered a sea storm which blew the young scholar to a strange land. The inhabitants on the land had long beards and spoke Chinese. After talking with them, the young scholar learned that he had accidentally landed in "the Kingdom of Long Beards." Afterwards, the king who ruled over the kingdom made the young scholar a top ranking official and betrothed his daughter to him. The scholar lived a very comfortable life there and enjoyed everything that came with his high position. One day, the king and his ministers looked worried and depressed. So, the scholar asked the king what had happened. "There will be a catastrophe here in the kingdom. I was wondering whether you could call on the Dragon King of the East Sea and inform him that the Kingdom of Long Beards, located on the Seventh Island and Third Branch, needs his help. Because our kingdom is too far away," the king wept, "could you earnestly plead with the Dragon King of the East Sea?" Not long after that, the king sent subordinates to accompany the scholar by ship. Within the blink of an eye, the scholar arrived at the East Sea.

The young scholar went to the East Sea Dragon Palace and introduced himself as an emissary of the Kingdom of Long Beards. When he said this, the Dragon King of the East Sea gave him a warm reception. After he had stated his case, the Dragon King immediately ordered his subordinates to look for the island. After searching for a

[1] Wu Zetian (AD 624 – 705) was a Chinese sovereign who ruled unofficially as empress consort and empress dowager and later, officially as empress regnant during the brief Zhou Dynasty (周 , AD 684– 705), which interrupted the Tang Dynasty (AD 618– 690 & 705– 907). For more than two millennia, Wu was the sole officially recognized empress regnant of China.

东南沿海一带的人们一旦遇到海事，就披发掷钱米，呼龙王以求救。这是因为有老渔民讲，一次出海的时候，众渔船才到水深处不久，天空忽然飘来一团巨大的黑云，海面上登时风起浪涌。离黑云较近的渔船转瞬间就被风浪掀翻，有的甚至连人带船被卷入空中。众人都吓呆了，这时不知谁喊了一声：“快向龙王求救！”慌乱中，大家纷纷跪倒叩拜，大呼“龙王救命”。有人还把随船带来的酒水食物一同丢进海中，恳求龙王收下。这时海面渐渐升起一个巨大的水柱，水柱之上站立一人。仔细看去，那人朱发长髯，头有犄角，穿鱼鳞金甲，着龙纹战袍，手持宝剑，高大威武。说来也怪，水柱上的人一现身，那团黑云便似畏惧一般向远处退去，风浪也随之平息。眨眼间，手持宝剑的人也消失了，海面上也没有了水柱。原本漂在海面的酒水食物，也找不到了。于是，渔民知道是龙王前来相救，那高大威武的身影正是南海龙王。

在四海龙王之中，记载最少的是北海龙王。他只和其他三位龙王一起出现过。但是这也并未妨碍北海龙王掌管一方海域，担负布云施雨的职责，而人们也敬其为一方海神，加以信奉。

在中国历史悠久的海洋文明中，四海龙王可以称得上是最接地气的海神。因为在诸多记载中，四海龙王并非一直以

while, a subordinate reported that there was no such kingdom in the East Sea. The scholar thought about the words the king had uttered, and pleaded with the Dragon King once again. He told him that the Kingdom of Long Beards was located on the Seventh Island and the Third Branch. The Dragon King of the East Sea had to order his subordinates to intensify their search. After a meal, the subordinate reported again: "the Kingdom of Long Beards is a shrimp island, and this month, they are expected to supply your food." The Dragon King of the East Sea laughed out loud then said: "So that's the way it is. Although I am the king of the East Sea, every month, the Kingdom of Heaven is responsible for providing my meals. I cannot catch fish and shrimps at will. But since you have interceded for them, I will show some mercy by reducing the amount of food provided this month." The Dragon King followed up his promise and ordered to release the Shrimp King and other shrimps back into the sea. He also dispatched guards to take the scholar home. The ship arrived in Dengzhou, Shandong Peninsula, overnight. When the scholar went on shore, the guards and ship vanished in an instant. Everything that had happened was just like a dream.

There are stories about the Dragon King of the West Sea rescuing drought-stricken people and the Dragon King of the East Sea helping the inhabitants of the Kingdom of Long Beards.Besides,the Dragon King of the South Sea also has his own stories.

During the Ming (AD1368-1644) and Qing Dynasties (AD1616-1911), people in the southeast coast had the habit of throwing coins and rice into the sea whenever they encountered shipwrecks. Simultaneously, they called upon the Dragon King to come to their help. They did that because of a

救苦救难的正面形象出现。虽然贵为一海之主，位列仙班，但是四海龙王却表现出和凡人一样的喜怒哀乐。在《西游记》中，东海龙王敌不过孙悟空，被夺去定海神针，最后只好向玉帝告状，一诉委屈。在《封神演义》中，东海龙宫三太子被哪吒抽筋刮鳞，东海龙王恼怒之下不顾百姓安危，水淹陈塘关，与哪吒斗法，败下阵之后无奈去向玉帝求援。在《观音全传》中，南海龙宫三太子被渔翁捕去，陷入险境，南海龙王无力相救，跪拜恳请南海观音施以援手。这些故事中，龙王有心怀愤恨告状之时，有罔顾百姓犯错之时，也有力不能及求助之时。这些表现实际上与海神的身份并不相符，反倒与凡人无异，但正是这一点，体现了人们在对龙王的信仰中所寄托的真切细微的感情，也使龙王得到了人们的喜爱，被广为信奉。回归到海神信仰的本身，四海龙王虽有着别样的人物特点，但是其降雨、应愿、护海的职责与功能在漫长的历史中并未发生变化，而这也是四海龙王成为海神的根本原因。

龙的形象并不只出现在华夏文明中。在西方文明中，龙也是一个很重要的角色，但是两种文明中的龙存在很大的差异。一方面，龙的形象大相径庭。在西方的描述中，龙一般长有巨翅、利爪，面部狰狞，口中会喷火伤人。另一方面，

story told by some old fishermen. Once upon a time, when they had just arrived at the deep sea in their fishing boats, the winds picked up and dark clouds began to gather in the distance. As they sailed closer to the clouds, their boats were overturned by stormy waves and some sailors were swept off the ground and thrust into the sky. The sailors were all frightened. One of them shouted, "Ask the Dragon King for help!" The sailors kowtowed in panic and yelled, "Please help us! Dragon King!" Some sailors threw food and wine into the sea and begged the Dragon King to accept their offer. At that time, a huge water column gradually rose on the sea surface. Above the water column stood someone. When they took a close look at him, they found that the tall man had red hair, long whiskers, two horns, gold scales, and a war robe in the pattern of a dragon and he was holding a double-edged straight sword. When the man appeared on the huge water column, dark clouds slowly drifted away, then the sea calmed down. In a flash, both the huge water column and the man were gone. However, the food and drinks that once floated on the sea surface could no longer be found. So, the sailors knew it was the Dragon King who had saved them. And that was exactly the Dragon King of the South Sea.

The Dragon King of the North Sea is the most mysterious. Even though he is only portrayed alongside the other three Dragon Kings, the Dragon King of the North Sea is just as capable as them in performing his duties. That explains why the common people piously worship him too.

In China's long history of marine civilization, the Dragon Kings of the Four Seas are the most human-like sea gods because they did not always appear in a positive image. Although they are the masters of the seas, the Dragon Kings of the Four Seas experienced similar joys and sorrows as mortals. In the novel *Journey to the West*, the Dragon King

龙王

of the East Sea could not defeat Sun Wukong[1]. Consequently, his Compliant Golden-Hooped Rod was taken away. He had no option but to complain to the Jade Emperor. As recounted in the novel The Investiture of the Gods, the third son of the Dragon King of the East Sea was killed by Nezha[2]. The Dragon King was so angry that he disregarded the safety of the locals and flooded Chentang Pass as he battled with Nezha. After he was finally defeated, the Dragon King ascended to the Kingdom of Heaven to present his case to the Jade Emperor. According to *Guanyin Biography*[3], the third son of the Dragon King of the South Sea was caught in a fisherman's net and taken away. Therefore, the Dragon King had to beg Guanyin of the South China Sea to rescue his son from the fisherman. In these stories, we can see that the Dragon Kings also had moments when they were aggrieved, enraged or helpless. The sense of powerlessness does not tally with the image of sea gods. However, it makes them more like mortals and accounts for the true and subtle feelings placed on them by people. That also explains why people love and respect the Dragon Kings so much. Every one of the Dragon Kings of the Four Seas has his unique characteristics, but their duties towards

[1]

Sun Wukong, also known as the Monkey King, appears as a main character in the 16th-century Chinese classical novel *Journey to the West* (《西游记》). In the novel, he is a monkey born from a stone who acquires supernatural powers through Taoist practices. After rebelling against the Heaven and being imprisoned under a mountain by the Buddha, he later accompanies the monk Tang Sanzang on a journey to retrieve Buddhist sutras from "the West".

[2]

Nezha (哪吒) is a protection deity in Chinese folk religion. His official Taoist name is "Marshal of the Central Altar" (中坛元帅). He was then given the title "Third Lotus Prince" (莲花三太子) after he became a deity.

[2]

Guanyin Biography depicts how Guanyin became a deity and includes stories about her and her disciples.

龙所代表的意义也存在很大差异。西方的龙并不是神，而是邪恶的代表，一旦出现就意味着灾难，喷火焚烧，荼毒生灵。在《圣经》中，龙发水成洪灾，企图冲走妇人并吃掉刚生下的孩子。它还鼓动怪兽征服人类，被认为是魔鬼撒旦的化身。不仅西方典籍记载中龙的形象如此，在西方当代的文学作品中，龙所代表的主要是邪恶和力量，这在《霍比特人》《冰与火之歌：权力的游戏》中都有所体现。

在中国的海洋文明中，四海龙王遨游于天地之间，布云施雨，实现祈愿，庇佑平安，是当之无愧的海神。正因为如此，人们对于四海龙王的信奉一直延续至今。而四海龙王所表现出来的烟火气，也使得他们不断出现在各种影视文学作品中，为人们所喜爱。如今，沿海地区还存有许多龙王庙，供人们敬奉香火。每逢休渔期结束，开海之际，人们还会举行声势浩大的祭祀龙王仪式，以寄托万事顺利、获得丰收的美好愿望。这正是中国海洋文明的一种传承。

rainfall, wish fulfillment and the protection of the seas remain the same. This is why the Dragon Kings of the Four Seas are ultimately considered as four sea gods.

The image of the dragon does not only appear in Chinese civilization. In western civilization, the dragon also plays a very important role, but the dragons in the two civilizations exhibit differences. In addition, the actual image of the dragon is quite different. The western dragon generally has giant wings and sharp claws. It is sinister in appearance and is capable of breathing fire. Furthermore, the meaning of the dragon is also different. In western countries, the dragon is not considered as a god. On the contrary, it symbolizes evil. It appears in times of disasters. In the Bible, the dragon caused floods, attempted to wash away a woman and eat her new-born baby. The dragon also incited monsters to destroy human beings. That is why it was considered as the incarnation of the devil, Satan. In both western classics and contemporary literary works, the image of the dragon mainly represents evil and power as reflected in *The Hobbit* and *A Song of Ice and Fire: Game of Thrones*.

In China's marine civilization, the Dragon Kings of the Four Seas are well-deserved sea gods. They are responsible for making rain and fulfilling people's wishes. Therefore, people have continued to believe in the Dragon Kings till this day. The Dragon Kings of the Four Seas also appear in different films, TV series and literary works and are deeply loved by the Chinese people. Today, there are many Dragon King Temples along the coastal areas for people to offer incense. Whenever the fishing season starts, people expect to have a rich harvest by holding a grand ritual in honour of the Dragon Kings prior to setting out to the sea. This is the inheritance of marine civilization.

张生煮海情比金

第五章

Chapter

Five

Scholar Zhang Boiling the Sea with Unwavering Love

爱情是一种可以穿越时空的力量，千百年来，人们执着于对爱情的追求，留下了无数动人的故事。古今中外文学作品中，爱情也一直是经久不衰的题材。无论是中国的《西厢记》《红楼梦》《白蛇传》，抑或是西方的《罗密欧与朱丽叶》《简·爱》《傲慢与偏见》，无一例外以爱情写就惊世名作。更有无数诗歌咏赞爱情，比如“在天愿作比翼鸟，在地愿为连理枝”“执子之手，与子偕老”“思卿至爱，心中便生财富无限，纵帝王屈尊就我，不与换江山”等。既然爱情是如此不朽的题材，在中国漫长的海洋文明中，这浓墨重彩的一笔自然不会缺席。其中最广为流传的，就要数张生煮海的故事了。

传说，广东潮州有个书生，名叫张羽，字伯腾。张羽自幼寒窗苦读，长大后却屡试不中。一日，他来到东海畔，忽见一座古寺，名叫石佛寺。寺中长老谈吐高雅，为人谦和，

Love transcends time and space. For thousands of years, a countless number of moving stories have been recounted by people . It is true at all times and in all counties- love has always been an everlasting literary theme. Whether it be *The Story of the Western Wing, The Story of the Stone, Legend of the White Snake* in Chinese literature, or *Romeo and Juliet, Jane Eyre, Pride and Prejudice* in the West, all of these are marvelous stories about love. Furthermore, countless poems praise love such as "on high, we'd be two love birds flying wing to wing; on earth, two trees with branches twined from spring to spring," "holding your hands and growing old together with you" and "for thy sweet love remember'd such wealth brings, that then I scorn to change my state with kings". Since love is such a universal theme, love stories have definitely been a part of China's long marine civilization. Here is the story titled Scholar Zhang Boiling the Sea with Unwavering Love, a story that is widely known across China.

According to the legend, a scholar named Zhang yu once lived in Chaozhou, Guangdong Province. He studied in straitened circumstances since he was a boy, and repeatedly failed the imperial examination. One day, Zhang went to the Stone Buddha Temple that stood over the East Sea. He met an elderly monk who had a refined way of talking and a modest and amiable nature. As a result, Zhang decided to live in the temple. On one clear moonlit night, Zhang got very lonely, so he decided to play heptachord in order to ease his loneliness. As he played, he could hear the melodious tweedle drifting away with the night breeze.

It so happened that Qionglian, the beautiful daughter of the Dragon King of the East Sea, was playing around there. She was completely overwhelmed by the melodious sound so she followed

张羽钦佩之余便借宿于寺内。一晚，张羽心中略起烦闷，而窗外月明星稀，万籁俱寂，越发使人寂寞。于是他取出素琴，于月色清空下轻抚起来。琴声悠扬，随风漾至远方。

事有凑巧，寺外东海之上，龙宫的三公主琼莲出海游玩，正来到此地。忽听得寺中悦耳琴声，如痴如醉，于是循声而去，一直来到了张羽的窗外。张羽正忘我弹奏，忽然琴弦“嘣”的一声断了。他心里一惊，想到必是有人偷听，赶紧走出门来。此时琼莲来不及躲避，仓促中两人相对而立。窘迫之下，琼莲只好说明，自己被琴声吸引，不觉来到此处。张羽心中微动，邀琼莲再听一曲。琴声流转之间，两人互生爱慕，临别之时约定八月十五在东海边相见。琼莲赠给张羽一条手帕，嘱咐说：“这块鲛绡手帕，就当作我的定情信物。”说罢，消失在门外。

然而，东海龙王得知此事后勃然大怒，他下令将三公主囚禁起来，派兵把守，不许任何人接近。可怜那张生对此一无所知，琼莲离开后，他再也无心读书，对着鲛帕，日思夜想。未及八月十五，便离开石佛寺，向东海边出发。张羽沿着东海边一直走，却始终没有找到琼莲。东海如此之大，琼莲到底在哪里呢？眼看着八月十五已经过去，他不禁心急如焚。

一日，他顺着山路来到一处断崖边，崖下是无边无际的

it to the window. Zhang was completely absorbed in his playing when suddenly, a weird string stroke. Zhang had a strange feeling that someone must have been eavesdropping, so he dashed out. Unfortunately for Qionglian, she had no time to hide. So, there they stood, Zhang and Qionglian, face-to-face. Because she was embarrassed, Qionglian had to explain that she was fascinated by the music. Upon hearing this, Zhang felt butterflies in the stomach and invited Qionglian to listen to another tune. He played the song so well that Qionglian fell in love with him. They planned to go on a date to the East Sea on August 15th of the lunar calendar. And before she was leaving, Qionglian presented Zhang a handkerchief as her pledge of love.

However, the Dragon King of the East Sea opposed their attempt of being together and imprisoned his daughter at the bottom of the sea. The poor scholar had no clue about what had happened. After Qionglian left, he held the handkerchief day and night, reminiscing about Qionglian. Zhang left the Stone Buddha Temple and gone to the East Sea before the day of their date. When August 15th of the lunar calendar finally came, Zhang could not find Qionglian. He walked along the East Sea in a vain attempt to find her. He asked himself over and over again where exactly she was. Zhang's heart was afire with impatience.

Zhang was completely overwhelmed with sadness as he walked to the coastal cliff one day. A Taoist nun walked out of a col and Zhang immediately asked her for directions. The Taoist nun replied by asking: "You scholar,why didn't you study for fame? Why did you come here?" Zhang narrated the events that had occurred prior to his meeting with

龙女

大海，已无路可循，张羽心中十分懊丧，不觉悲从中来，坐在一块圆石上直叹气。这时从山坳里走出一位道姑，张羽连忙上前问路。谁知那道姑并不回答，却反问道："你个书生，不读书考取功名，跑到这山野之地来做什么？"张羽原原本本将在石佛寺与琼莲相遇之事说了一遍。道姑听了，大笑道："你真是个书呆子。你所说的琼莲正是东海龙王的三公主，你一个凡人怎能与她婚配呢？况且，那东海龙王脾气暴烈，必然阻拦，我劝你，还是趁早回去吧。"

一番话，把张羽听得目瞪口呆，他哪里想到琼莲竟是东海三公主，心中更加悲戚。道姑见张羽一片真情，被他打动了。原来，这道姑叫作毛女仙姑，原是秦朝时的一名宫女，机缘巧合下得道成仙。只见毛女从袖袍中取出一只银锅、一枚金钱、一把铁勺，对张羽说道："我赠你三件宝物。你只需带着宝物到海边去，用铁勺舀一锅海水，把小钱扔在银锅里，架起火来煮即可。只要水一开，东海龙王便坐不住了。"

张羽来到沙门岛，捡了几块石头把锅支上，便依法煮起海水来。锅里的水"咕嘟咕嘟"开了，海水竟也像开了似的直冒泡。不一会儿，海面上出现了几个人，个个捧着金银珠宝，请求张羽停止煮海，张羽摇摇头，说什么也不肯停止。过了好一会儿，只见几名侍女扶着一个端庄白净的女子缓缓

the Taoist nun. The nun chuckled: "You are really a nerd. Qionglian is the daughter of the Dragon King of the East Sea. How can you a mortal marry a fairy? No mention the Dragon King has a bad temper. It's impossible for him to marry his daughter to you. You'd better follow my advice, and go back home now."

Zhang was astounded to hear these words. His sadness welled up. Fortunately, the Taoist nun was moved by the extent to which they loved each other, so she made up her mind to help Zhang. It turned out that the Taoist nun named Mao Nü was formerly a maidservant in the palace during the Qin Dynasty (221–206BC), and, by chance, had become immortal. In order to succeed, Zhang had to make the Dragon King come out of the sea. To help him do this, Mao Nü gave Zhang a silver pan, an iron ladle and a gold coin. She explained to Zhang how to use these three tools: On the coast of Shaman Island, he only needed to heat the pan over some stones and ladle in sea water; when the pan was full he had to put in the gold coin and quickly bring the water to boil. She told him that when the water in the pot was hot, the sea water would be hot too, and when the water in the pot boiled, then the sea water would boil as well.

When Zhang did this, it caused the sea to boil. After a while, several people holding treasures appeared on the sea and requested Zhang to stop boiling the sea, but he refused. Finally, the Dragon King had no choice but to compromise. So, he sent Qionglian back to Zhang. The lovers could finally get married. The Dragon King betrothed his daughter to Zhang and he also organized a grandiose wedding for them.

Because they were faithful to each other, Zhang and the Princess of the East Sea ultimately had a happy ending. But as a famous line goes, "men have sorrow and joy; they part or meet again; the moon is bright

走来，那女子梨花带雨，纤细娇柔，不是琼莲又是谁？原来，龙王在海中热得无处逃躲，别无他法，只得依了他二人姻缘。几日之后，水晶宫里张灯结彩，为张羽和琼莲举行了隆重的婚礼，这对有情人终成眷属。

张羽和东海三公主因彼此的忠贞而获得了圆满的爱情。但是人有悲欢离合，月有阴晴圆缺。有的爱情注定无法圆满，那些有着缺憾的爱情，虽承载了苦涩，却也有着别样的美丽，比如青龙石和白虎山的故事。

传说青龙星本是东海龙宫里的侍卫将军，他对上有令则行，对下有求必应，还常常救百姓于苦难之中，因此广受百姓敬奉。一次，玉帝下旨要在东海龙宫中挑选一名得力将军到天宫任职。龙王忍痛割爱，将自己最得意的青龙将军送上了天宫。

青龙星上天之后被封为凌霄宝殿的执殿将军，每日恪尽职守。因常在凌霄宝殿，他渐渐与王母娘娘身边的一位侍女白虎星产生了爱慕之情。两人约定，趁王母娘娘举办蟠桃盛会之际，一起逃出天宫，私奔凡间，永结同好。等到这一天，二人好不容易溜出了瑶池，却在南天门被四大金刚拦住了去路。玉帝得知他二人私奔，当即震怒，下令将青龙星贬回东海，又将白虎星罚到凡间，令二人永世分离，不得相见。

or dim and she may wax or wane." Some love stories are destined to have regrets. Sad as they may be, they also possess unique beauty. And the story of Azure Dragon Rock and White Tiger Mountain is a case in point.

According to the legend, Azure Dragon Star was the general of the guards in the Dragon Palace of the East Sea. He granted both the Dragon King of the East Sea and the mortals whatever they requested . In addition, he regularly relieved people from their sufferings. Once, the Jade Emperor announced that a qualified captain needed to be selected from the Dragon Palace of the East Sea to hold a post in the Kingdom of Heaven. Following the announcement, the Dragon King chose and dispatched Azure Dragon Star, his favorite general to fill the position.

Henceforth, Azure Dragon Star became the general in Lingxiao Palace, a duty he fulfilled conscientiously. He gradually fell in love with White Tiger Star, a maid of Queen Mother of the West[1]. Then they planned to elope during the Feast of Peaches[2] organized by Queen Mother. Unfortunately, when the day came, they were blocked by four Heavenly Guardians in the Southern Gate when they had just slipped away from the abode of the Queen Mother.When the Jade Emperor heard about the attempted escape, he thundered and reacted by exiling Azure Dragon Star to the East Sea. He also made sure that the lovers were separated forever by sending White Tiger Star to the mortal world.

When Azure Dragon Star came back to the Dragon Palace, the

❶

Queen Mother of the West: the ruler of the western paradise and keeper of the Peaches of Immortality.

❷

The Feast of Peaches: Every six thousand years, Queen Mother of the West has a birthday celebration which is called the Feast of Peaches. The date for the festival exactly coincides with the ripening of the immortal peaches.

青龙星回到东海龙宫后，龙王怕触怒玉帝，不敢再重用他，只派他当了一个推潮神。做推潮神枯燥费力，但青龙星也从未出过差错,唯一的苦楚就是思念被贬入凡间的白虎星。

再说白虎星被贬至镇海一个官宦人家当了侍女。一次，镇海发大水，白虎星落水，随波浪漂浮，最后被风刮到了岱山岛的沙滩上。等她醒来后才知道，原来是当地的土地神救了她。土地公公同情她的处境，便偷偷告诉她，青龙星自从被贬回东海，就在这一带做推潮神。白虎星感激之余，匆匆赶去与青龙星相会。

白虎星与青龙星久别重逢，互诉衷肠，二人既高兴又伤心。谁知此事很快传到了龙王耳中，他怕玉帝怪罪自己，当即下令将白虎星镇在岱山岛西北面的一座山下，这座山后来就叫作“白虎山”，而青龙星则被镇在岱山岛东南面的一块礁石下，这块礁石弯弯曲曲，远远望去，活像一条石龙，当地百姓就把这块礁石称为“青龙石”。从此白虎星与青龙星就只能隔岛相望，再无法相会。

爱情里有圆满也有缺憾，但无论是圆满还是缺憾，都少不了与磨难抗争。在今天我国的环北部湾地区，还流传着一个“珠还合浦”的感人故事。

从前，合浦县白龙湾海底出产稀世珍宝夜明珠。白龙湾

Dragon King of the East Sea made him a simple Tidal God, because he did not want to enrage the Jade Emperor by giving him an important position. Even though the work of a Tidal God was both dull and demanding, Azure Dragon Star never made a mistake. But he missed the White Tiger Star all the more.

After her exile to the world of the mortals, White Tiger Star became a maid in the family of a public official. One year, the entire village was flooded. White Tiger Star also fell into the flood and was washed up on the beach of Daishan Island. When she woke up, she found that it was *Tudigong*[1] who had saved her. *Tudigong* sympathized with her predicament, then told her that Azure Dragon Star lived nearby as a Tidal God. Fortunately, after a long separation, they finally reunited.

However, when the Dragon King heard about the reunion, he trapped White Tiger Star under a mountain in the northwest of Daishan Island. Because he was afraid that Jade Emperor would blame him. Consequently, the mountain under which White Tiger Star was trapped became known as White Tiger Mountain. For his part, Azure Dragon Star was trapped under a rock in the southeast of Daishan Island. Because the rock under which he was trapped looked like a stone dragon, it was called Azure Dragon Rock. Ever since, White Tiger Star and Azure Dragon Star can only see each other across the island but can never meet.

Whether perfect or imperfect, love is always accompanied by struggles. Around the Northern Gulf Areas of China, there is another touching story.

Once upon a time, luminous pearls were produced in Bailong Bay, Hepu County. Generations after generations of people who lived in Bailong village made their living by collecting pearls. Haisheng, a

[1]

Tudigong, also known simply as *Tudi* (土地 "Soil-Ground") in Chinese folk religion, is a tutelary deity of a locality and the human communities who inhabit. .

附近有一个渔村叫白龙村，这里的人世世代代靠采珠过活。村子里有个叫海生的青年，是个采珠能手。一天，他出海采珠时遭遇守珠的恶鲨，他与恶鲨搏斗，身负重伤，危难之际海里出现一位姑娘，对他施手相救，海生这才得以脱身。

原来那姑娘是夜明珠化成的珍珠公主，她同情珠民，又爱慕勤劳勇敢的海生，于是化身渔女，来到白龙村，与海生结婚生子，并指点珠民采珠。因为有了珍珠公主的指点，珠民们总能大获丰收。不久，白龙湾海底有夜明珠的消息不胫而走，传到了皇帝那里，皇帝十分贪心，派太监到白龙村，强迫珠民下海采捕夜明珠。那太监非常凶恶，不仅要挟珠民采珠，还威逼珍珠公主交出元神夜明珠，否则便血洗渔村。珍珠公主无奈之下只得离开亲人，还身变回夜明珠。

太监得到夜明珠后，连夜动身赶往京城。到了梅岭下，太监开箱查看，却发现箱内空空如也，夜明珠早已不知去向。皇帝知晓后，龙颜大怒，处死了太监，又派了一位太监前往合浦索珠。有了上次的教训，这次来的太监忍痛割开自己的大腿，将夜明珠藏于其中，以防丢失。回程行至梅岭地界时，霎那间天昏地暗，惊雷四起，一道闪电冲破黑暗袭来。太监大惊，割开大腿一看，夜明珠又不见踪影。此刻，合浦海面珠光灿烂，百姓高呼：合浦珠还！皇帝得知神仙显灵后，怕

young man, was proficient at fishing for pearls. One day, when he was working, a shark attacked and seriously injured him. Lucky for him, at that precarious hour, a beautiful woman showed up and rescued him.

As a matter of fact, the woman was a Pearl Princess, the very incarnation of a luminous pearl. Because of her sympathy for the villagers and her admiration for industrious and brave Haisheng, the Pearl Princess turned into a fisherwoman, married Haisheng and helped the villagers to fish for pearls. With the help of the Pearl Princess, villagers constantly had a bumper harvest. Before long, the greedy emperor heard that luminous pearls existed at Bailong Bay, so he sent a eunuch to the village. The vicious eunuch forced the villagers to fish for pearls. He also threatened the Pearl Princess to hand over her luminous pearl to him. The Pearl Princess had no choice but to leave her family and transform back into a luminous pearl.

The eunuch decided to return to the capital overnight as soon as he had got the legendary luminous pearl. However, when he opened the box on his way back, the pearl disappeared. The emperor flew into a rage and killed the eunuch. Then he sent a second eunuch back to the village. Judging from what had happened earlier, the second eunuch cut open his thigh and hid the pearl in it to prevent it from missing again. On his way back, suddenly, a gust of wind darkened the sky and everything got obscured after a sudden clap of thunder. The eunuch cut open his thigh and found that the pearl had disappeared again. At that moment, the sea sparkled with a shining light. It was the pearl returning once more to Hepu County again! For fear of offending deities, the emperor finally gave up the idea of capturing the pearl. After that, the Pearl Princess turned back into a fisherwoman and together with Haisheng, lived happily ever after.

得罪神灵，终于放弃夺取夜明珠的念头。此后，珍珠公主再次化身渔女，与海生过上了美好幸福的生活。

中国海洋文明中有许多爱情故事，从上述三个故事中，我们能看到“情比金坚”的爱情如此美丽与可贵。这些林林总总的故事，也融进了人们生活，产生了深远的影响。比如张生煮海的故事，早在元代就已经被写成杂剧，后又编成越剧。青龙石和白虎山的故事则在岱山岛地区世代相传，寄托着人们对爱情的期许。合浦珠还的故事不仅载于书中，还衍生出大量的民间故事。以合浦珠还为题材的文学艺术作品也丰富多彩，比如北海南珠碑林、大型粤剧《珠还合浦》、合浦大型根雕《珠还合浦》、连环画《夜明珠》以及大量的诗歌、音乐舞蹈作品等。人们用各种各样的方式去记录和还原这个传说，也正是希望爱情永恒，犹如蔚蓝的大海中生生不息的朵朵美丽浪花。

China's marine civilization is filled with love stories. From the three stories above, we can see that love is beautiful and valuable. These stories have also become a part of people's lives and have had far-reaching effects on them. For example, the story of Scholar Zhang Boiling the Sea with Unwavering Love was written as a *Zaju*[1] as early as the Yuan Dynasty (AD1206-1368). Later, it was composed as a Shaoxing *opera*[2].

The story about White Tiger Rock and Azure Dragon Mountain has been passed down from generation to generation around Daishan Island. The Hepu Pearl story has not only been documented in the form of a book but has also inspired a large number of folk stories. There are many literary and artistic works with the theme of the return of Hepu Pearl such as Forest of Steles of Beihai Nanzhu; an important Cantonese opera[3] Return of Hepu Pearl ; large-scale tree-root carvings, anda comic strip *Legendary Luminous Pearl* and other poetic and choreographic works. People have adapted this legend in many ways and genres in the hope for love that will last forever just like the beautiful everlasting waves in the sea.

❶

Zaju (杂剧) was a form of Chinese drama or opera which provided entertainment through a synthesis of recitations of prose and poetry, dance, songs, and mime, with a certain emphasis on comedy (or, happy endings). Originating in the Song Dynasty, it has particularly been associated with the time of the Yuan Dynasty, and remains important in terms of the historical study of the theater arts as well as Classical Chinese literature and poetry.

❷

Shaoxing opera, also known as Yue opera (越剧), is the second most popular opera form out of over 360 opera genres in China. Originating in Sheng County (嵊县), Zhejiang Province in 1906, Yue opera features actresses in main roles, as well as femininity in terms of singing, performing, and staging. Over time, it grew in popularity. Only Peking opera is more popular. It is highly popular in Zhejiang, Shanghai, Jiangsu and Fujian, while its audiences are all over China.

❸

Cantonese opera (粤剧) is one of the major categories in Chinese opera, originating in southern China' s Guangdong Province. It is popular in Guangdong, Guangxi, Hong Kong, Macau and among the Chinese community in Southeast Asia. Like all versions of Chinese opera, it is a traditional Chinese art form, involving music, singing, martial arts, acrobatics, and acting.

鲛人泣珠报恩德

第六章

Chapter

Six

Legends of Jiaoren Shedding Tears of Gratitude

数千年来，人们一直在探索蔚蓝的海洋，海洋却一直保持着神秘。伴随探索而留下来的，是无数的海洋神话传说，其中最为神秘的要数鲛人的故事。鲛人的存在既不同于各种海洋神明，又区别于各类水中精怪。书载：鲛人，鱼之灵异者。居住于海洋深处，鱼尾人身，性情温和。男性鲛人背上有角质鳍，女性则是透明软质。这里我们就主要讲讲其中几个故事。

传说茜泾地区有个叫景生的人，在闽地客居三年后，乘海船返乡。船中途停靠时，他看到沙滩上躺着一个人，无法动弹。那人生的碧眼蜷须，浑身漆黑。景生好奇，就上前询问。那人回答说："我是海底鲛人，原本为水晶宫琼华三姑子织紫绡嫁衣，因出错弄断了九龙双脊梭，被流放到此。我如今漂泊无依，如果您能收留我，我必将报答您的恩德。"景生听了，心生同情，救下鲛人作为仆从，一同归乡。这鲛

For thousands of years, people have explored the ocean, but the ocean has remained mysterious. That's why there exist countless myths and legends all centered on the ocean. The myths of *Jiaoren* feature among some of the most intriguing. A *Jiaoren* is neither a sea god nor a monster. Ancient Chinese books have it that *Jiaoren* are supernatural creatures that live among fish. They live deep in the ocean, and have a fish tail, a human body and a mild temperament. Male *Jiaoren* have cutin fins on their backs, while female ones have transparent and soft fins. There are multiple stories about Jiaoren.

Once upon a time, there lived a man in Xijing. His name was Jingsheng. He went away on a voyage to Fujian Province where he lived for three years. On his return, when he docked his ship, he saw a man lying motionless on the beach. The man had blue eyes, curly hair and a dark skin. Jingsheng was curious. He walked up to the man and the man said, "I am *Jiaoren* from the ocean. I used to sew purple silk wedding clothes for Jade Third Sister-in-law in the Crystal Palace. But I was exiled here because I mistakenly broke Kowloon Double Ridge Shuttle. I am homeless now. If you can take me in, I will repay your kindness." Jingsheng felt sympathetic, so he rescued the Jiaoren and took him home. Jingsheng found that *Jiaoren* did not have any hobbies neither did he have any talents. The only weird habit he had was to go to the pond after dinner and have a bath. And he did this day in and day out. Apart from the shower, he generally just crouched in one corner, had no expression on his face and did not say anything to anyone. Jingsheng did not like this but, at the same time, did not feel like asking him to leave.

At one time during the Yufo Festival, Jingsheng decided to go to the Epiphyllum Temple. In the crowd there, he saw an old woman in the company of a refined and delicate young woman. Jingsheng fell in

鲛人

love with the young lady at first sight. Later, he learned that the young lady was from Wu State (parts of present-day Jiangsu and Zhejiang provinces). Her name was Tao, and her nickname was Wanzhu (meaning ten thousand pearls). She had moved to this area with her widowed mother three years earlier. Without further delay, Jingsheng paid her a visit and asked to marry her. Unfortunately, Tao rejected his request. Her mother told him, "Since my girl's name is Wanzhu. If you really want to marry her, you must offer ten thousand pearls."

Dejected, Jingsheng returned home. The thought of not being able to obtain ten thousand pearls, even if he sold all he had, made him gloomy day and night. Consequently, he took ill. After the doctor's diagnosis, Jingsheng was informed that he had lovesickness, a disease that had no cure. Some days later, he was so sick that he thought he would die. At that time, *Jiaoren* came to visit his master. Jingsheng said to him, "I am afraid that I'm going to die for love. Where would you go when I die? " When *Jiaoren* heard this, he was sad too, so he burst into tears. Then, all of a sudden,

人既没有什么嗜好，也没有才能。只是每日饭后必到池塘洗浴，然后就蹲在角落里，面无表情，一言不发。景生心中不悦，但也不忍把他赶走。

一次浴佛日，景生到昙花讲寺去看热闹。人群中，景生看到一老妇人带着一位妙龄女子参拜。那女子清丽脱俗，纤柔娇弱。景生一见倾心，随后打听到那女子本是吴人，姓陶，小字万珠，三年前，随寡母迁居到此。景生随即登门求聘，却遭到拒绝。老妇人告诉他："小女名叫万珠，必得万颗明珠，方能应命。"

景生失望而归，想到明珠万颗，纵然耗尽家财也难以凑齐，因而日夜愁闷，不久就病倒了。医生诊断他得了相思病，无药可治。又过了一些日子，景生病得瘦骨嶙峋，奄奄一息。鲛人知道后，来看望主人。景生说道："我怕是要为情而死了，你跟我才半年。一旦我先死去，你又到哪里去呢？"鲛人听到这番话，悲从中来，不禁失声痛哭。景生低头发现地上跳落许多珍珠，每一粒都如佛宝如意珠般光洁饱满，原来是鲛人的眼泪化成了明珠。景生的病顿时痊愈，将求娶陶氏女一事悉数告诉了鲛人。鲛人将明珠拾起数了数，不到一万颗。景生问道："不能再试着哭一下了吗？"鲛人回答说："我们鲛人哭笑，由心而发，不像这世间的人，动辄以假面

Jingsheng saw a large number of pearls jumping up and down on the floor. Each of them was bright and each of them was full. As it turned out, *Jiaoren*'s tears could transform into pearls. Jingsheng immediately recovered, then he explained to *Jiaoren* why he had become ill. *Jiaoren* picked up all the pearls on the floor, yet they were not enough. So, Jingsheng said to *Jiaoren*, "Could you try to cry again?" *Jiaoren* answered, "No, I can't." Unlike humans, whenever *Jiaoren* cried, it came from the heart. He could not fake his emotions. "If you really want pearls, take wine to the Sea View Tower tomorrow, I will give you more pearls." he recommended.

The following morning, Jingsheng took wine to the Sea View Tower. He went with *Jiaoren*. The hazy misty could be seen floating on the sea as the horizon appeared to separate the sky from the water. *Jiaoren* drank a cup of wine which provoked an overwhelming feeling of homesickness. Then he broke down into tears. As a result, pearls started raining on the floor. Jingsheng hastily picked them up, then he assembled them in a jade plate which he held out saying, "These are enough." But *Jiaoren* replied: "When I get this emotional, I just can't stop." So, he cried on till he had no tears left. Jingsheng was very happy and he asked *Jiaoren* to come home with him. However, pointing at the east, *Jiaoren* laughed and said, "The Chicheng sunglow has appeared. Today is the day when Jade Third Sister-in-law marries Immortal Diaoao in the Coral Island. It's the end of my banishment. I am leaving." Then he jumped into the water and disappeared leaving Jingsheng to return home alone.

The next day, Jingsheng went to the Tao family. He had with him ten thousand pearls and was ready with a marriage proposal. The old woman was surprised and said, "You are truly in love with

孔示人。如果您想要，那就明日带我携酒登望海楼，让我来凑齐明珠吧。”

翌日清晨，景生携酒和鲛人登上望海楼，只见烟波浩渺，水天一线。鲛人取杯自饮，看着大海，思乡情起，不觉泪珠迸落。景生赶紧用玉盘盛起来，说道：“这就够了。”鲛人却回道：“忧从中来，不可断绝。”于是纵情大哭，泪尽方止。景生十分高兴，邀鲛人一同回去。鲛人却指着东方笑着说：“赤城霞出现了。琼华三姑子今天下嫁给珊瑚岛钓鳌仙史。我的灾限已满，自此与你分别！”说罢，纵身一跃，消失在海水中。景生只好怅然独返。

次日，景生取出明珠，去陶家下聘。老妇笑说：“公子真是痴情人。我不过以此相试，岂能真卖闺女，以此谋取生活？”因此，拒绝了景生的明珠，将女儿嫁给了他。后来景生与万珠生了一个儿子，取名梦鲛，以纪念鲛人帮助他们结成姻缘。

鲛人于灾限之中，仍泣珠报景生搭救之恩，是为真情。虽能泣珠，却仍哭笑由心，是为真性情。真性情者予人以真情，这一鲛人泣珠的故事令人感动之余，也发人深思。不过，鲛人泣珠的故事并不只这一个，《博物志》中就另有记载。

有一次，一个鲛人女子来到海边的一户人家求宿，说道：

my daughter. But I was just trying to test you, how could I really sell my daughter to make a living?" Therefore, she refused the pearls and married her daughter to Jingsheng. Later, the couple had a boy whom they named Mengjiao (meaning dreaming of *Jiaoren*) as a tribute to *Jiaoren*, who had helped them tie the knot.

In return for saving his life, *Jiaoren* offered pearl tears to Jingsheng. And despite his ability to produce pearls by crying, *Jiaoren* still demonstrated profound and genuine feelings. This was *Jiaoren*'s true disposition. People with genuine sentiments treat others without disguise, and *Jiaoren*'s story is a case in point. The story is heart-warming as well as thought-provoking. More stories have been told about *Jiaoren* including the one in the ancient book *Records of Myriad Things*.

According to the story, there once were beautiful Jiaoren-like type of women. Despite their lovely features, they had no feet. Their skin was as white as jade. Their lower bodies had no scales but just fine, colorful and soft hair. Their hair, like that of ordinary women, was tied into pony tails. One day, one of the women went to a seaside residence and asked for accommodation. She said, "I am *Jiaoren*. I can weave silk and I can keep it dry even when it is soaked in water. The clothes made out of the silk are of great value. If you let me live here, I will weave silk for you in exchange." When they heard this, the family decided to take her in. Although *Jiaoren* looked like humans, she constantly stayed in the water and spent her time weaving silk. Each time she finished weaving a piece of silk, the home owner took it to the market and sold it. The family made a fortune selling the silk. However, one day, when the house owner was about to take the new silk to the market, *Jiaoren* came out of the water and asked for a tray. Then she burst into tears. The owner was surprised to find that the tears *Jiaoren* shed had transformed

“我本鲛人，善织鲛绡。鲛绡入水而不湿，可以成服，价值百金。我愿织鲛绡，以求收留。”于是这户人家收留了她。鲛女虽外貌与人无异，但常浴于水中，织作鲛绡。每成一匹，就由家中主人拿到集市中去售卖。这样过了一段日子，这户人家以鲛绡换得了诸多钱财。但是，突然有一天，家中主人正要将新的鲛绡拿到集市上去售卖,鲛人女子却从水中出来，索要了一个托盘，随即痛哭流涕。这家主人惊讶地发现，鲛人女子所落泪滴皆化为明珠，落在托盘之中。眼看托盘盛满了明珠，鲛人女子停止哭泣，将明珠递与主人，就此拜别。她出门入海，再不见踪影。这家主人此时才明白，鲛人女子是泣珠报恩。后来，这一故事就流传开去。

据载，福建厦门有一对夫妇，以出海打渔为生。一次出海，有一条丈许的大鱼撞上渔船，渔妇就用船篙去驱赶大鱼，大鱼却昂首向渔妇跃起，如此三次才入水离去。事后，渔妇常常梦到和大鱼交合，不久之后竟怀孕了。分娩时，产下的男婴外表就像鱼皮一样。但这个孩子常常感到身体发痒，一旦发痒就要闭门洗浴。有一次，夫妇二人从门缝偷偷看去，只见孩子竟然像一条鱼一样在浴盆中游动。虽然故事里没有明确说夫妇之子为鲛人，但鱼化而为人，极有可能是鲛人。《徂异志》中也记载有人见过鲛人。书中写道：宋朝有个名

into pearls as they rained unto the tray. When the tray was full of pearls, *Jiaoren* stopped crying. She handed the tray to the home owner and left. She went out of the house and jumped into the sea. The owner then realized that *Jiaoren* cried pearls to express her gratitude. Later, the story went viral.

Apart from the story about shedding tears of gratitude, there are also other legends about *Jiaoren* in ancient Chinese books. There is a story about a couple in Xiamen, Fujian Province who made a living by fishing in the sea. One day, when they were fishing, a big fish smashed unto their boat. The fish was over three meters long. The woman used her paddle to drive the fish away. The fish didn't go away immediately. It jumped out of the water three times, then swam away. After that episode, the woman consistently dreamed about engaging in sexual encounters with the big fish. Before long, she was pregnant. When she gave birth, she found that the baby boy's skin was exactly like that of the fish. The woman's first instinct was to abandon the baby. However, her husband insisted on keeping him. From that day, the number of fishes they caught increased. Over the years, they were able to save some money as the child grew up. However, the baby regularly felt physically itchy and each time he did, he closed the door and washed his body. Once, the couple peeked through the door and unexpectedly found the boy swimming in the tub like a fish. In the story, it is not clearly indicated that the boy was *Jiaoren* but there is every reason to believe he was because he was the child of a fish.

According to the record of another ancient book, an official in the Song Dynasty (AD960–1279) named Zha Dao was dispatched as an envoy to Goryeo (an ancient country in the Korean Peninsula). He arrived one evening and docked his ship near the shore. He and his companions found a woman on the beach. She was dressed in red, had

叫查道的官员，奉命出使高丽，傍晚时分所乘船只靠岸停泊。众人发现沙滩上有一个妇人，穿红色衣服，袒露双臂，臂肘后部有红色的鱼鳍，且发髻凌乱。查道命令船工不要伤她，用船篙将其扶到水中。那妇人入水之后，没入水中又现身，向着查道拜谢施礼。这妇人正是海中鲛人。

在中国的海洋文明中，鲛人虽有美丑之分，但都知恩图报，因此才有了种种鲛人泣珠的故事。在西方的海洋文明中，有关鲛人的记载也有很多，但是西方习惯于把鲛人称为美人鱼，其形象几乎都是美丽女子。鲛人与美人鱼最重要的区别在于，早期西方的美人鱼往往与海妖同义，会魅惑水手，导致海难发生。古希腊神话中的人鱼形象是海妖塞壬。塞壬是河神埃克罗厄斯的女儿，是从他的血液中诞生的美丽妖精，因为与缪斯比赛音乐落败而被缪斯拔去双翅，无法飞翔。失去翅膀后的塞壬只好在海岸线附近游弋，有时会变幻为美人鱼,用自己的音乐天赋吸引过往的水手使他们遭受灭顶之灾。德国的传说及诗歌，则常提及美丽人鱼罗蕾莱。她经常会在天色昏暗的时候出现在莱茵河畔，用她冷艳凄美的外表以及哀怨动人的歌声迷惑过往的船夫，使其分心而迷失方向，最后沉入河底。

后来西方的文学中，逐渐出现了美人鱼和人类男子相爱

bare arms, red fins at the back of her elbows and her hair was a tangled bun. Zha Dao instructed his boatmen not to hurt her and he helped her back into the water. Once back in the water, the woman reappeared and bowed to Zha Dao. This woman was *Jiaoren* from the sea.

In China's marine civilization, there are both beautiful and ugly *Jiaoren*. However, they are similar in their display of gratitude to people who help them and they always reciprocate whenever there is an opportunity. That is why there are many stories about *Jiaoren* shedding tears . In Western marine civilization however, *Jiaoren* are known as mermaids. In addition, they are all represented by the image of beautiful women. The most important difference between Chinese *Jiaoren* and Western mermaids is that the early Western mermaids were the same as sirens who bewitched sailors and caused shipwrecks. In ancient Greek mythology, the image of the mermaid was the siren. She was the daughter of Achelous, the river god, and she had the blood of her father by virtue of her birth. Siren was defeated by Muse in a music contest and, as a result, she lost her wings and could fly no more. From that day, Siren could only swim near the coastline and she sometimes transformed into a mermaid and use her charming voice to lure passing sailors, then wreck their ships. German legends and poems often refer to the beautiful mermaid Lorelei, who used to appear on the banks of the Rhine at dusk. She enchanted passing boatmen with her glamorous physical appearance and her sorrowful songs, and caused them to lose direction and eventually sank with their boats.

The image of mermaids was boosted by stories that appeared later in western literary works about them falling in love with and marrying humans. One of the most widely known stories is the mermaid princess

和结婚的故事，美人鱼也有了正面的形象。其中最广为人知的就是安徒生笔下《海的女儿》中的人鱼公主。故事中，小人鱼公主浮出海面远望人间，恰好救下了落水的王子，并且爱上了他。为了陪伴心爱的王子，人鱼公主失去了美丽的歌喉，化为人形后，宁愿忍受刀割般的疼痛也要为王子跳舞，但最终王子还是与邻国公主结婚，而人鱼公主则化为海上的白色泡沫。她选择用自己三百年的寿命换取对爱人的成全和一个纯洁的灵魂。故事中的小人鱼公主美丽而惹人爱怜，无论是作为人鱼还是作为人类，她的灵魂都像透明的海水一样纯洁。这个故事，在此后百余年间感动了世界上无数的人，也使得人鱼为更多人知晓。

无论是中国海洋文明中泣珠的鲛人，还是西方海洋文明中凄美的人鱼，始终神秘而美丽，并且对中西方文学和文艺作品的创作，产生了巨大的影响。比如，三国时曹植有诗《七启》，其中写道："采菱华，擢水苹，弄珠蚌，戏鲛人。"后至唐，李商隐在《锦瑟》中写下的千古名句"沧海月明珠有泪，蓝田日暖玉生烟"，所用典故正是鲛人泣珠。后代历朝文学作品中都有鲛人出现，志怪杂记中更是多到难以计数。在现当代文学作品中，鲛人或是人鱼往往是虚幻类小说创作的重要素材，有的还被拍摄成影视

in *The Daughter of the Sea* by Andersen. In the story, the mermaid princess emerged from the sea to see the world. She found that a prince was drowning, so she saved him. They eventually fell in love. The mermaid princess had to lose her beautiful voice and transform into a human in order to be together with her beloved prince. She also endured immense pain to dance with the prince. Unfortunately for her, the prince eventually married the princess of a neighboring country abandoning the mermaid princess who then turned into foams on the sea. She had sacrificed her 300 years of existence so as to fulfill her love. She, therefore, had a very pure soul. The mermaid princess in the story is beautiful but pitiful. Whether as a mermaid or a human being, her soul is as pure as the transparent sea water. For more than a hundred years, this story has touched countless people and, at the same time, it has made mermaids a favorable figure among humans.

Jiaoren in Chinese marine civilization and the mermaid in the Western marine civilization are always mysterious and beautiful. They have had a tremendous impact on both Chinese and western literature works. For instance, the famous talent Cao Zhi in the Three Kingdoms Period (AD220–280) wrote a poem titled Qiqi which, among others, reads "picking water chestnuts, lifting water plants, collecting unionid, and playing with *Jiaoren*." Then in the Tang Dynasty (AD618–907), the renowned poet Li Shangyin wrote the much-quoted lines in his poem "The Sad Zither": "Tears that are pearls, in ocean moonlight streaming; Jade mists the sun distils from Sapphire Sword." The poems allude to the legends of *Jiaoren* shedding pearl tears. The image of Jiaoren also appeared in literary works throughout later dynasties, and even more ubiquitous in all kinds of strange stories. In modern and contemporary literary works, *Jiaoren* or mermaids are often an important

作品，出现在荧幕之上。除了拍成电影，西方的美人鱼故事也多次被改编成舞台剧，深受人们喜爱。虽然中西方对鲛人和人鱼的叙述存在差异，但是与之相关的故事却始终寄托着人们对未知海洋的期许。也许我们的后人千年之后，还会继续吟唱："南海有鲛人，深水居如鱼，不废织和绩，滴泪能成珠。"

source of fiction, and some have been adapted to films and television series. Besides, the western mermaid stories have been adapted to stage plays which a lot of audience enjoy. Although there are differences in the description of Chinese *Jiaoren* and western mermaids, all of the stories underlie human expectations of the unknown ocean. And probably a thousand years later, our descendants will continue to sing the famous lines:

> There are *Jiaoren* in the South China Sea,
> Living like fish in the deep sea,
> Endlessly weaving silk,
> And shedding tears of pearl.

第七章

妈祖仁爱写传奇

Chapter

Seven

The Legends of Mazu with Great Humanity

今天，在中国的东南沿海、日本以及新加坡、马来西亚、泰国等东南亚国家，人们共同信奉着一位能够守护平安、消灾避祸的海神，她就是妈祖。与传统海神有所不同的是，妈祖是由真人真事演变而来，最初是民间传说，后经过历史化和神化，才逐渐形成了广泛的妈祖信仰。作为一位广受人们敬奉的海神，妈祖博爱仁慈而又勇敢无畏，她扶弱济贫，铲除邪恶，留下了许多传奇的故事。

据记载，妈祖是五代时闽王统领军兵马使林愿与妻子王氏所生的第六个孩子，原名林默。林默出生之时，天降红光，屋内光辉夺目，弥漫着久久不散的香气。屋子四周隆隆作响，好似春雷轰鸣，大地也在一片轰鸣声中变成了紫色（紫色代表祥瑞）。伴着诸多奇异景象，王氏产下一女婴，但女婴满月之前无一声啼哭，因而得名“默”。

生于异象，注定了林默的不凡。她聪慧过人，又异常勇

Today many people worship a sea goddess who can safeguard peace and chase away evil spirits. Her name is Mazu. The belief in Mazu is widespread on the southeastern coast of China, in Japan and other Southeast Asian countries including Singapore, Malaysia and Thailand. Unlike other traditional sea gods, Mazu evolved from a real person. She is the deified form of a purported historical figure. People in her hometown had profound love and respect for her. Mazu was fearless and kindhearted. She exorcized evils spirits and helped the poor. That's why there are many legendary stories about her.

Mazu was the sixth daughter of Lin Yuan, the chief military inspector during the period of the Five Dynasties (AD907–960). Her original name was Lin Mo. When Lin Mo was born, a flash of red light shot from the sky and illuminated her room. Then a lingering fragrance permeated the air. The house appeared to be rumbling like spring thunder. The earth turned purple (in China, purple represents auspiciousness). It was in this mysterious context that Ling Yuan's wife gave birth to a baby girl. During her first month of life, she did not cry aloud like other infants. Therefore, she was given the name Mo (which means "silent").

The auspicious circumstances were a clear indication that Lin Mo was destined to be extraordinary. As she grew up, it soon became apparent that Lin Mo was gifted with remarkable intelligence and bravery. She also excelled in swimming and astronomy. Rumors ascribed her mystical powers due to an event that took place when she was sixteen. One day, Lin Mo was out enjoying a stroll with her close friends. She stopped to check her makeup in the reflection of a well. At that moment, an immortal emerged from the water holding two bronze

妈祖

amulets. He offered them to the girls. Terrified, all the girls, except Lin Mo, ran away. She calmly accepted the amulets. The immortal received her as a disciple. From then on, Lin Mo became increasingly powerful. She could transform herself into various shapes and forms, cast magical spells, and ride clouds across the ocean. Wherever there was a shipwreck, she showed up and rescued those involved. So, out of respect, people called her "the Magical Lady" and "the Daughter of the Dragon".

During the Song Dynasty, foreign trade along the coastal line thrived. Unfortunately, there were frequent shipwrecks because the technology was outdated, and boats were rudimentarily designed and built. At that time, there was a sea monster called Yan Gong who took pleasure in overturning ships for fun. His action brought ineffable suffering to the locals.

One day, when Lin Mo was sailing on the sea, Yan Gong began to stir up huge waves. Lin Mo's ship shook violently and was about to capsize. Then Lin Mo asked the people sailing with her to anchor their ship at the shore. She told them she was going to combat the sea monster alone. The smug sea monster was wearing a red robe and a golden crown. He had a black face with thick eyebrows. He used sorcery to stir up violent waves. Lin Mo drew on her supernatural powers and stirred up one mountainous wave after another to fight against Yan Gong. Frightened, Yan Gong grudgingly withdrew. The monster then turned into a dragon that was over thirty meters long and continued to wreck boats. But Lin Mo was determined to subdue the cruel beast. Therefore, she cast magical spells and ended up capturing Yan Gong, the dragon. Afterward, Lin Mo was designated as the commander of Sea Guardians, and later during the Ming Dynasty

敢，加上在海边长大，她还通晓天文，熟习水性。林默十六岁的时候，有一天和要好的姐妹们结伴出游。在一眼水井边，她正对着井水照妆时，一位仙人从井中缓缓升起，手中持有一对铜符。林默的姐妹们见此景象，惊慌中纷纷逃离。而林默却镇定地跪拜仙人，接受铜符，并学习仙法。此后，林默的仙法日益精进，能够通灵变化、施咒辟邪，甚至呼风唤雨。她还常常乘云游弋于海上，遇到遭遇海难的人们，则出手搭救。于是，人们渐渐就称呼她为“神姑”“龙女”。

宋朝时期，沿海地区对外贸易十分兴盛，但由于技术落后，船舶简陋，海难时有发生。那时，海上有一个叫作晏公的精怪，常常掀翻过往船只，人们苦不堪言。有一天，林默乘船到了海上，晏公又开始兴风作浪，林默所乘船只剧烈摇晃，眼看就要倾覆。这时，林默让人停船下锚，自己去对付晏公。一片海浪中，只见一个身穿红袍、头戴金冠的人正在施法，他长得浓眉虬髯，面如黑漆，脸上尽是得意之色。林默见此，开始施展神通，掀起一波又一波的滔天巨浪，次次压过晏公。晏公因此产生畏惧，悻悻地叩拜离去。但他离开后转而化为一条数十丈长的恶龙，继续施法，想要掀翻船只。这次，林默决心彻底降服晏公，于是施展神通，缚住恶龙。晏公终于心悦诚服地认输。后来，晏公做了水阙仙班的统领，

(1368–1644), she became a worshiped deity.

In addition to the above stories, there are other legends about her benevolent exploits. The legends include how she defeated other sea monsters, prayed for rain and prevented floods. Therefore, the locals held Mazu in great reverence. All the experiences fortified her will and mind. She was no longer the same young girl who had initially acquired these extraordinary powers. This transformation also heralded her forthcoming metamorphosis.

Lin Mo's ascension, at the age of 28, was as remarkable as her birth. The day before the Double Ninth Festival, Lin Mo calmly said to her parents and siblings, "I'm going to celebrate the Double Ninth Festival on the hill tomorrow." None of them had any idea that she would become a deity and would lose her physical self forever. The following morning, Lin Mo bid farewell to her family and ascended the hill, the highest point on Mei Zhou Island. When she reached the summit, Lin Mo was encircled by dense fog. In the company of enchanting celestial rhythms, she was carried into heaven by a golden glowing light. A brilliant rainbow appeared where she had been last seen (In Chinese mythology, the rainbow signifies great blessings and good fortune). Henceforth, Lin Mo has been a sea goddess. It is said that the cliff where the four words "Sheng Tian Gu Ji" (Relics of Ascension) are carved was the exact spot where Lin Mo ascended to heaven and became an immortal.

After becoming an immortal, she did not stop looking out for mortal beings. She frequently came to the aid of sailors and fishermen in trouble.

In October, 1682, Shi Lang (AD1621–1696), commander-in-chief of the Chinese navy, leading 30,000 sailors stationed in Pinghai

到明朝时也成为守护一方、受人敬奉的神祇。

除了窥井得符、降服晏公，林默还曾收服海怪嘉应与嘉佑、祈雨济民、解除水患，为百姓做了很多好事，因此百姓对她越发崇敬。这一切更磨练了林默的意志与心性，她已然不再是当初那个初学仙法的少女了，这也预示了即将到来的蜕变。

林默二十八岁那年，重阳节的前一天，她对家人说："我心中向往清净，要离开凡尘喧嚣。明天是重阳佳节，我想去爬山登高，特地和你们告别。"家人都以为她只是要登高远眺，却不知道她将要飞升成仙。第二天早上，林默焚香诵经之后，告别亲人和好友，独自登上了湄峰。等林默到了湄峰的最高处，天空中传来祥瑞之音，并出现五彩祥云，她踏上祥云，冉冉升入高处，再无踪迹。至此，林默飞升成仙，真正成为一方海神妈祖。据说如今湄峰妈祖庙后的摩崖"升天古迹"就是妈祖飞天的地方。

归入仙班之后，妈祖虽然远离了尘世的喧嚣，但从未忘记凡间众生，她多次显灵，于是又有了这样的故事。

传说康熙二十一年十月，清军水师提督施琅奉旨率三万水兵驻扎在莆田平海镇，等待乘风东渡收复台湾。当时正遇到干旱，军中缺水，施琅十分焦虑，因此向妈祖祈祷。妈祖

town, Putian, Fujian Province, attempted to recapture Taiwan. While waiting for the wind to blow in their direction and facilitate their sail , his troops ran short of water. Shi Lang became anxious, so he turned to *Mazu* for help. *Mazu* instructed him to reopen an abandoned well near Thean Hou Temple. So, Shi Lang ordered his troops to do so. As they expected, sweet clear water flowed out of the well. Shi Lang carved the word "Sacred Water" beside the abandoned well to show his appreciation to the goddess for mercifully dispensing water from the well. Till date, sweet water has continued to flow from the well. That same year, on the night of December 26th, Shi Lang led the troops across the sea and for the first time, launched an attack against Taiwan and Penghu Islands. But without the wind, the gigantic warships moved very slowly. When he missed the opportunity to attack the enemy, he ordered his sailors to return to Pinghai. Unfortunately, on their way back, there were strong winds which caused many boats to either sink or simply disappear. However, all lost boats were miraculously found the following day. They were docked at Meizhou Bay. A soldier reported to Shi Lang that the previous night, they had seen a light near the warships and they felt like someone was picking up the lost boats. The soldier believed it must have been *Mazu*. Shi Lang was greatly touched when he heard what *Mazu* had done. So, he ordered his subordinates to renovate Thean Hou Temple in Pinghai and rebuild *Mazu*'s statue. He also made significant donations toward the building of Shuzhuang Tower and Chaotian Temple. In addition, he enshrined a statuette of *Mazu* on his ship. The following June, Shi Lang attacked Penghu Islands for the second time. Later, when being asked why they were so brave in combat, some soldiers claimed that

指点施琅，只要挖开天后宫旁被填的废井就可以解决缺水的问题。施琅命令属下照办，井中果然流出了甘甜的清水。施琅感念于神赐甘泉济师，亲自书写“师泉”二字，这口井保留至今，甘甜的井水也从未枯竭。同年的十二月二十六日夜，施琅第一次率兵渡海攻打台湾和澎湖列岛，但是因为没有海风，硕大的战船行进缓慢，施琅因为失去了战机而下令回航平海。可就在回航后不久，海上突然刮起大风，战船上有很多小艇被刮下海，不知去向。第二天风停后，所有丢失的小艇均已安稳地停在湄洲湾中。士兵向施琅报告说：昨晚在风浪中看到战船不远处有亮光，亮光之中好像有人在收揽被吹落的小艇，有这样神通的一定是海神妈祖。施琅大为感动，命令整修平海的天后宫，重塑妈祖神像，捐重金建梳妆楼、朝天阁，并请回妈祖神像一尊奉祀在战船之上。次年六月，施琅第二次率兵东渡攻打澎湖，军中士兵感到神妃在左右助战，个个英勇无比，奋力作战。当时，军中千总刘春梦到天妃告知二十一日必然攻克澎湖，七月必然攻克台湾。后来清兵强攻澎湖七昼夜，并最终统一台湾。这就是甘泉济师、佑助收艇和澎湖助战的故事。

此外，据记载，乾隆二十一年二月至二十二年正月，全魁和周煌奉命出使琉球。在途中正好遭遇了风暴，当时狂风

骤雨愈演愈烈，船只剧烈颠簸，船上摔倒呕吐的人数众多。全魁和周煌于恐慌之中多次向海神妈祖祈祷，妈祖给出指示："宁泊于此，毋舍去也。"众人听从妈祖的指示，在风浪中苦苦支持。等到十天之后的夜里，海上再次狂风大作，船上的桅杆和弦索全部断裂，并触到了礁石，船舱瞬时涌入大量海水。虽然离海岸只有六七百步远，但在狂风暴雨中，众人已陷入绝境。就在危急时刻，桅杆上出现了光亮，妈祖随之现身，并开始结印施法。于是从漆黑的海面飘来一朵朵花一样的灯光，每个人都被一团灯光包裹，随后妈祖挥动衣袖，众人便随着灯光漂向岸边。在登上海岸之后，大家纷纷虔诚地向妈祖叩拜。经历此劫，人们无一不感叹妈祖救人于海难中的神力和她庇护百姓的仁爱。

无论是成仙之前的林默，还是成仙之后掌管水阙仙班的妈祖，一直尽心尽力、守护大海子民，这是一种仁爱；降服海怪、助阵统一，这是一种正义；不畏艰险、消除海难，这是一种勇敢。仁爱、正义、勇敢的妈祖的信仰，代表的是人们对和平、宽容与和谐的追求，这也正是妈祖精神最核心的内涵。

今天，在妈祖诞生地福建莆田的湄洲岛上，矗立着著名的湄洲祖庙，而在福建省的泉州也建有泉州天后宫。虽然妈

Mazu had appeared and supported them in their endeavor. Liu Chun, an admiral, dreamt that Mazu had told him that they would conquer Penghu Islands on July 21st, and then recapture Taiwan in July. After struggling for seven days, the soldiers conquered Penghu Islands and eventually unified Taiwan.

Historical accounts have it that, Quan Kui and Zhou Huang, in their capacity as Chinese ambassadors, visited Ryukyu from February 1756 to January 1757. Their ships encountered a windstorm and were at the point of sinking. Many people on board had seasickness as the ship rocked in the wind. Panicking, Quan Kui and Zhou Huang repeatedly prayed to Mazu who responded by saying: "You'd better stay here than abandon the ships." Everybody took Mazu's advice as they fought through the storm. Ten days later, there was yet another violent storm. It was so strong it tore through the mast and rigging. This time around, the ships crashed onto a reef causing the hull to flood with water. They were only nine hundred meters away from the coast, but the situation of the sailors was precarious. At that critical moment, a bright light appeared on the horizon and Mazu showed up to rescue them. The flower-like bright light enveloped every sailor and with a wave of her sleeve, Mazu helped them to drift ashore. They bowed to Mazu after the rescue. People marveled at Mazu's divine power and were touched by her benevolence.

Whether she was Lin Mo, an ordinary person or Mazu, a goddess, she devoted herself to protecting the people. These stories reveal her benevolence, sense of justice and courage. The stories also foreground people's aspiration for peace, mercy and harmony, which underlies the very essence of Mazu.

祖最初只是闽粤一带海洋信仰的神明,但是随着时间的推移,妈祖信仰也随着华人的足迹而传遍世界各地。例如在台湾社会中，妈祖信仰已经成为主要的民间信仰，台湾大大小小的妈祖庙已远远超过一万座，其中规模较大的有鹿港天后宫、鹿耳门圣母庙、北港朝天宫、台南大天后宫等。妈祖阁又称为妈祖庙,是澳门最著名的名胜古迹之一,至今已逾五百年。四百多年前，葡萄牙人抵达澳门，于庙前对面之海岬登岸，注意到有一间神庙，询问居民当地名称及历史，居民误认为是指庙宇,故此答称“妈阁”,葡人以其音译而称“MACAU”,成为澳门葡文名称的由来。因此，澳门别名是“妈祖”，就是葡萄牙人对澳门的最早称谓。与此同时，在世界其他各国也有着数以万亿计信仰妈祖的人。现在，在新加坡、马来西亚、泰国、印度尼西亚、日本等国都有供奉妈祖的寺庙，如马来西亚的青云亭、宝山亭，新加坡的天福宫等。此外，有关海神妈祖的小说、电视、电影、动漫等也不断问世，为人们所称道。这既是对以妈祖为代表的海洋文化的传承，也是对中国传统文化的弘扬，将激励后人不断在广阔的海洋中探索新天地，追求更美好的未来。

The famous Meizhou Temple now stands on Meizhou Islands in Putian, Fujian Province, which is the birthplace of Mazu. Similarly, Quanzhou Thean Hou Temple is located in Quanzhou, Fujian Province. Mazu was originally a sea goddess in the coastal areas of Fujian and Guangdong provinces. As time went by, the belief in Mazu spread throughout the world. For example, in Taiwan, Mazu is an important goddess and the local people believe in her. There are more than ten thousand Mazu temples in Taiwan alone. The biggest ones include Lugang Mazu Temple, Luermen Mazu Temple, Beigang Chaotian Temple and Tainan Grand Mazu Temple. In Macau, one of the most attractive scenic spots is Mazu Pavilion, otherwise known as Mazu Temple. This temple has a history of over five hundred years. When the Portuguese landed on the shores of the sea opposite the temple four hundred years ago, they asked the local residents for the name and history of the region. The residents mistakenly thought they were asking about the temple, so they replied "Ma Ge"(Mazu Pavilion). The Portuguese recorded this as "Macau" and that is how Macau came into being. That is also the reason why Mazu is a nickname for Macau. In addition, numerous people in other countries believe in Mazu.

Today, many countries including Singapore, Malaysia, Thailand, Indonesia, Japan all have Mazu Temples, such as Qingyun Temple and Baoshan Temple in Malaysia, and Tianfu Temple in Singapore. Novels, television shows, movies and animations about Mazu continue to emerge and receive acclaim. They center around the inheritance of marine culture as they equally promote traditional Chinese culture. And these traditions will continue to encourage future generations to explore the unknown in their pursuit of a better future.

第八章

八仙过海显神通

Chapter

Eight

Eight Immortals Crossing the Sea

中国的海洋神话传说中，关于海神和海中精怪的故事最多，而在这些故事之外，也有一些别有趣味的异闻传说，在民间广为流传。有一首歌谣唱道：“钟离宝扇自摇摇，拐李葫芦万里烧。洞宾挂起空中剑，采和一手把篮挑。张果老人知鼓道，湘子横吹一品萧。国舅曹公双玉板，仙姑如意立浮桥。”歌谣中的人物正是道教八仙，我们要讲的就是八仙过海的故事。

历史上，八仙的说法起初并不统一。明时，铁拐李、钟离权、张果老、蓝采和、何仙姑、吕洞宾、韩湘子、曹国舅八人利用仙法，在民间扶危济困，留下各种故事，被称为道教八仙。今天，流传最广的正是道教八仙，而他们施法渡海，各显神通的故事最为人津津乐道。

传说西王母蟠桃盛会之后，八仙行至东海，停云观望。只见潮头汹涌，巨浪滔天。吕洞宾言道：“今日乘云而过，

Among Chinese marine myths and legends, stories about sea gods and goblins are the most predominant. In addition to these stories, there are also interesting anecdotes that are popular among the people. A ballad goes like this: "Zhongli Quan swings his fan, Li Tieguai holds his fire gourd, Lü Dongbin levitates his sword, and Lan Caihe controls his basket. Zhang Guolao is a master drummer, and Han Xiangzi plays the flute. Cao Guojiu uses his double jade boards, and He Xiangu stands on a floating bridge". It features the Eight Immortals of Taoism and the following story is about them.

There are different versions of how the Eight Immortals originated. Today, the most popular version hails from the Ming Dynasty (1368–1644), when Li Tieguai, Zhongli Quan, Zhang Guolao, Lan Caihe, He Xiangu, Lü Dongbin, Han Xiangzi and Cao Guojiu were called the Eight Immortals of Taoism. In Chinese mythology, the Eight Immortals were a legendary group of eight individuals who transcended human forms and were endowed with divine powers. As a result, people take delight in telling the story of how the Eight Immortals reveal their divine powers while crossing the sea.

As the story goes, the Eight Immortals went to the East Sea after attending the Feast of Peaches. At the sea, they watched gigantic waves surging one after another. Lü Dongbin suggested that each of them should show their "magical power" by crossing the sea with just one thing. All the other immortals agreed with him. Then, one by one, they threw down their personal tools and transformed them. Li Tieguai threw his iron crutch down from the cliff. As soon as it touched the surface of the water, it transformed into a small wooden boat. Li Tieguai sat in the boat and could easily cross the sea. Zhongli

不见各家本事。试以一物投之水面，各显神通而过如何？”众仙纷纷赞同，各自施展神通。铁拐李即以铁拐投水中，好似木舟，自立其上，乘风逐浪而渡。钟离权以芭蕉扇投水中，扇子大如蒲席，平稳而渡。张果老以纸驴投水中，骑纸驴踏水而渡。洞宾以宝剑投水中，御剑而渡。韩湘子以箫管投水中而渡。蓝采和则将花篮投水中，坐花篮而渡。仙姑将荷花置于海面，立于花朵之上而渡。曹国舅以玉板投水中而渡。

海底龙宫之中，东海龙王正在与群臣议事，忽见水面一派白光，照耀水晶诸宫，透明天地。龙王不知何故，急令太子摩揭探视。太子得令，立即带领虾兵蟹将，绕海巡视，只见海面之上蓝采和乘坐花篮，浮海而过。魔揭太子道：“我在龙宫，万宝俱备，未见如此物之奇妙可爱者，不如使人夺之。”于是命令一众虾兵蟹将前去抢夺宝物。蓝采和突然之间被虾兵蟹将团团围住，立即施法反击，但无奈寡不敌众，最后不但失了花篮，自己也被抓到海底去了。再说魔揭太子将蓝采和囚在幽室，持宝归宫。一时宫殿光明，如添日月，龙王大喜，设宴庆贺。

众仙登岸后，独不见蓝采和，便让吕洞宾前去找寻。洞宾前往海滨遍寻不得，乃高声叫曰：“龙王好好送人还我，

Quan followed. He slung his fan down into the sea. The fan grew into a gigantic sheet that tided him over the torrents. Close behind, Zhang Guolao cast down his paper mule, He Xiangu threw down her lotus, Lü Dongbin used his sword, Han Xiangzi transformed his bamboo flute, Lan Caihe manipulated his flower basket, and Cao Guojiu used his jade boards. The Eight Immortals all landed on the surface of the sea and displayed their supernatural powers as they crossed the sea.

The Dragon King of the East Sea was holding a council in his palace when a bright patch on the surface of the water caught his attention. It illuminated the roof tiles of his crystal palace. This was weird, so the King immediately dispatched his son, the Dragon Prince to find out what had happened. The Dragon Prince assembled a group of soldiers and led them to the surface, so they could look around. They saw only Lan Caihe floating on the water with his flower basket underfoot. The Dragon Prince thought to himself, "There are many precious objects in my palace, but nothing is like this beautiful, strange and rare thing. I want it." Then he ordered his soldiers to attack. Suddenly being surrounded by so many soldiers, Lan Caihe had no chance of winning. He was captured and locked up at the bottom of the sea while his flower basket was seized and taken to the Dragon King. When the Dragon King saw the flower basket, he knew it was an object of great value. Out of delight, he ordered that preparations should be made for a great feast in the Dragon Palace.

Meanwhile, when the other immortals reached the shore, they realized that Lan Caihe was missing. Lü Dongbin looked for him along the shore but he could not find him. So, he stood on the shore and shouted: "Dragon King, listen to me! If you return Lan Caihe to me, I will forgive you; but if you don't, I will set a fire that will dry up your

如其不然，举火烧干汝海。”魔揭太子大怒，即出海面与吕洞宾对骂，且口出狂言，始终不肯还人。吕洞宾大怒，拔剑赶去。魔揭太子并未与之相敌，而是复入水中。吕洞宾乃把火葫芦投入海中，须臾变出千百葫芦，烧得水面皆红，海中鼎沸。至此，龙王才命左右送蓝采和上岸，与洞宾相见。吕洞宾收了葫芦，携蓝采和离去与仙友重会。

却说众仙见蓝采和、吕洞宾皆至，欣喜无限。唯蓝采和涕泪潸然，细说端由，恳请众仙友为其报仇，言讫大哭。众仙皆怒，商议之下，使吕洞宾再往龙宫索取花篮。洞宾乃同仙姑再往，大声索取。魔揭太子大怒，带领虾兵蟹将来擒吕洞宾。吕洞宾与战数合，太子败走海中。何仙姑施法困住太子。吕洞宾大喝一声，将剑望空一掷，正中太子头额而杀之。

败兵报知龙王，言魔揭太子被杀。龙王大惊，急令二太子来战。何仙姑、吕洞宾挺身力斗。忽见二太子把枪一招，海中兵将四面围裹将来，把吕洞宾、何仙姑团团围住，一时冲突不出，吕洞宾着急，忙取飞剑望空掷去，化作万千长虹，从天飞落，杀得四面围兵，血花飞溅，死者无数。二人冲出阵前，正遇二太子挺枪纵马来到，洞宾拔剑一挥，生生断其左臂，二太子负痛逃入海中，余兵俱皆逃命。吕

sea." The Dragon Prince had sharp ears, so he could hear Lü Dongbin. He was infuriated by what he heard. He raced to the surface and rudely refused to return Lan Caihe. Lü Dongbin was furious as well. He took out his precious sword and brandished it at the Dragon Prince. The Dragon Prince was no match for him, so he escaped into the sea. Lü Dongbin followed him. He put his fire gourd into the sea and it multiplied a thousand times. And every gourd immediately set forth a current of hot air that, began heating the sea. In the palace, the Dragon King got hotter and hotter, but there was no place to hide. He had to dispatch his soldiers to escort Lan Caihe back to the shore. When Lü Dongbin saw Lan Caihe, he retrieved his gourd and accompanied him back to the other immortals.

Once reunited, the immortals were all happy except Lan Caihe. He sobbed, "My precious flower basket is still with them. In my life as an immortal, I had never imagined suffering this kind of humiliation. My fellows, you must help me." So, they began to discuss ways of retrieving the flower basket. Again, they decided that Lü Dongbin should go and ask the King to return it. He Xiangu accompanied Lü Dongbin out on the sea. They shouted for a long time, and again, aroused the Dragon Prince. When the Dragon Prince appeared with his soldiers, Lü Dongbin charged forth to combat them. The Dragon Prince was again defeated. Unfortunately, when he wanted to flee, He Xiangu blocked his way and Lü Dongbin accidentally killed him.

When the Dragon King heard that the Dragon Prince had been killed, he was shocked. Immediately, he ordered the Second Prince to fight the immortals. He Xiangu and Lü Dongbin again got ready for battle, but, this time, the Prince's martial abilities were extraordinary.

吕洞宾龙太子

He surrounded them with countless soldiers, making it impossible for them to escape. Lü Dongbin looked around quickly, then he threw up his sword and chanted an incantation. Suddenly, the sword transformed into thousands of flying blades which killed numerous soldiers. The two immortals walked out triumphantly and confronted the Prince. Lü Dongbin cut off the Prince's right arm. The Prince let out a cry and jumped back into the sea. At the same time, the Dragon King just heard the news. When he saw the severed arm of the Prince and heard that most soldiers had been killed, he shouted out sadly and then fell onto the ground. When he recovered, the King ground his teeth and said, "So, Lü Dongbin, you have killed one and hurt another of my sons. If I do not revenge, I can't continue to be the ruler of the East Sea."

After he came back, Lü Dongbin and He Xiangu told the other immortals what had happened to them. Before long, the Dragon King mustered a force consisting of 100,000 soldiers ready to combat. Donning his own full uniform, he led his troop to the battlefront, cursing Lü Dongbin as he led the charge and declaring his intention to revenge the death of his prince. Zhongli Quan saw the Dragon King coming, then he led the way to confront the king's forces from the flanks. The Dragon King was already waiting impatiently, so when Zhongli appeared, he was spurred by the burning hatred and charged forward with his spear. The two enemies clashed over fifty times but neither of them succeeded to outperform the other. As the forces of the water clans saw that the Dragon King could not defeat Zhongli Quan, they closed in to help. When Zhang Guolao saw this, he realized that Zhongli was in trouble. He hoisted a signal flag summoning the other immortals. The Dragon King was quite taken aback. He was unsure

洞宾、何仙姑亦自退去。彼时龙王正在等候消息，忽见二太子断臂而回，大叫一声，昏厥于地。龙王醒后，悲愤欲绝，尽起海中十万精兵，亲自督战，誓要扫除仙党，以报二子之仇。

却说吕洞宾、何仙姑回见众仙，备言龙王不还宝物，反令其子统兵来战，被二人杀其长子，又断其二子一臂，败兵逃入海中。不久，果见尘头蔽日，喊杀连天，龙王引兵来到，列成阵势。龙王出阵，大骂吕洞宾，欲报二子之仇。八仙随即布阵与战，钟离自作先锋，舞剑出到阵前。龙王见了，更不答话，提枪直取钟离。二人战至五十余回合，不分胜负。众水军见龙王无法打败钟离权，便近前帮忙。张果老见了，摇动号旗，众仙从四面杀到，龙王不知四面之兵多少，其兵不战而乱，自相践踏，死者无数，龙王只得奔入海中。铁拐李、吕洞宾放出葫芦之火，烧干海水，烟焰腾天，须臾之间，东洋火炽，竟成一片白地。

东海龙王大败，携妻儿投奔南海而去。见到南海龙王敖钦，不禁痛声大哭，诉说了前后缘由。敖钦听后大怒，决心报仇，急令写告急文书二纸，以达西、北两龙王，并定下计谋，约以来日五更，准听连珠号炮，决水灌八仙，将其淹死在东海龙宫。西、北二王接得文书，开看一遍，令来使回报，

how many soldiers were attacking them. The Eight Immortals battled fiercer and fiercer, killing countless water clan soldiers. The Dragon King realized that he could not come out victorious, so he retreated. When the immortals saw the old Dragon King retreat, Li Tieguai and Lü Dongbin let loose the fire from the gourds. And it did not take long for the entire sea to dry up.

The Dragon King of the East Sea had to take his wife and sons to the South Sea. When the Dragon King of the South Sea learned about this, he was incensed and quickly came out to receive his brother into his palace. Then when he heard the lamentation of his kinsmen, the Dragon King of the South Sea felt the urge to do something. He devised a plan which consisted of combining all the water in the three remaining seas and using it to drown the Eight Immortals in the East Sea. The Dragon King of the East Sea and his brother of the South Sea set about implementing their plan of revenge. They sent emergency messages to the Dragon Kings of the West and North Seas, instructing them to wait for a signal (the sound of fireworks) at exactly five o'clock the following day, and to release water at the same time into the East Sea to inundate the Eight Immortals. Forty officials were also ordered ready their armies for the ensuing battle.

Meanwhile, the Eight Immortals, having conquered the Dragon Palace of the East Sea, were quite satisfied with their victory. All around them laid strange and wonderful precious objects. When they inspected the back of the palace, they found the flower basket that Lan Caihe had lost. They were all happy. However, at five o'clock, they suddenly heard a thunderous rumbling voice from above. Before they knew what was happening, a monstrous wave of water engulfed them. Luckily, Cao Guojiu's imperial board could break up

来日灌水伺候，惟听号炮进发。敖钦得了二处回音，乃令河海水官四十员，各带领兵去，接应四面之水，一切准备妥当，只待五更进发。

八仙烧干东海，夺得龙宫，见其中富贵非常，珍宝满地。入后宫后寻得蓝采和所失宝物，众仙大喜。五更时分，外面有炮声隆隆作响，众仙大惊，出视，只见四面潮头，滚滚而来。八仙急欲登岸，并无去路。正在惊慌，只见曹国舅一人不溺，行即水开，往即水止。众视之，其腰间宝带，乃辟水犀所制。众仙大喜曰："执此可复此仇矣。"乃各取其犀带一片在手，水即分开一路，众仙登岸逃出。

八仙逃至海岸，思量返去，难忍这口恶气。于是决定推倒泰山以填东海。于是八仙竟上泰山，先将余土沙石搬入东洋，然后八人分作八面，齐力将泰山一抬，震天响了一声，那山倒入海中去了，须臾间沧海变成桑田。八仙拍掌大笑曰："此可雪耻矣。"视之良久，乃投龙华会而去。

八仙虽胜，却不知东海龙王已上表天廷，告八仙毁泰山、塞东海的罪行。玉帝阅表，勃然大怒，即命大将赵元帅勘视。元帅领旨，往东海而来，只见泰山成地，东海成田。元帅随即率众天兵，往龙华会而来。却说八仙正在龙华会上，同众仙饮宴，忽门外喊声大起。赵元帅立马提刀，高叫："玉帝有命征讨，八仙可急向

the water and it enabled them to escape.

After surviving the disaster, the Eight Immortals cursed the four Dragon Kings. And the more they thought about it, the angrier they became. Then they were determined to teach them a lesson. So, they combined their powers and moved Mount Tai[1] to fill the East Sea. In an instant, the vast sea turned into a wide land. The Eight Immortals laughed and said, "This is real revenge!" After watching what was happening for a while, they left.

The Eight Immortals might have been victorious but the Dragon King of the East Sea had written a letter to Heaven in which he informed the Jade Emperor that the Eight Immortals had not only killed his son but also destroyed the whole East Sea. The Jade Emperor was extremely angry when he read the letter. Consequently, he dispatched his soldiers, led by General Zhao, to arrest the Eight Immortals. The Eight Immortals were enjoying a great feast when suddenly they heard screams from outside. General Zhao said to the immortals, "I have been ordered by the Jade Emperor to arrest you. Now, simply surrender and let the heavenly court punish you!" The Eight Immortals turned pale at the news but they were unwilling to receive the punishment, so they combated against the soldiers. At that point, Guanyin came to reconcile them. As soon as the holy deity came, all of them ceased their attack and kowtowed to her. The goddess of mercy smiled and pointed her finger to the East Sea. Then suddenly, Mount Tai that had destroyed the dragon's dwelling was lifted and

❶

Mount Tai (泰山) is a mountain of historical and cultural significance located north of the city of Tai' an (泰安), in Shandong Province, China. It is known as the eastern mountain of the Five Great Mountains of China. It is associated with sunrise, birth, and renewal, and is often regarded the foremost of the five. Mount Tai has been a place of worship for at least 3,000 years and served as one of the most important ceremonial centers of China during large portions of this period.

前受缚勿迟，不然刀斧无情。”僵持之下，观音菩萨飘然而至，出面调和。于是，天兵退去，龙王与八仙休战。随后，观音菩萨入海中一挑，把那泰山挑起，放在原处，海中殿宇景物恢复如故。玉帝关云一望，见泰山益高，东洋益深。乃召八仙、龙王曰：“汝等无故扰乱乾坤，本当重罪；但看在老道、老佛分上，并皆从宽，龙王罚俸一年，八仙谪降一等，俱限一年满足复常。”八仙、龙王谢罪拜别。自此天渊迥别，天下太平。

八仙过海各显神通的故事，世代流传，有着深远的影响。在中国历史上，有关八仙的文学艺术作品比比皆是，古代建筑中也多有八仙故事的雕刻彩绘等装饰，甚至在旧时新娘出嫁喜轿上，都可以看到形态各异、栩栩如生的八仙造型。明代的青花瓷瓶上有八仙为西王母祝寿的图案。在民间，有一种常见的家具被称为“八仙桌”。凡此种种，说明八仙在中国传统文化中具有深刻的影响力。今天，山东省蓬莱市有国家 5A 级景区——八仙过海景区，在这里游客能够切身体会到八仙过海这一神话传说的魅力。各种基于八仙过海故事改编的影视作品也时常出现在荧幕之上，深受广大观众的喜爱。由此可见，八仙过海的传说，对我国的民俗文化产生了深远影响，并逐渐形成了涉及艺术、宗教、文学等诸多领域的庞大体系，是中国海洋神话传说中的一块瑰宝，光彩夺目。

moved back to its original place. When the Jade Emperor saw Mount Tai and the East Sea restored, he smiled and then called up the Eight Immortals and the Dragon King of the East Sea to the Heaven. As punishment, the Eight Immortals were demoted by one level while the Dragon King's salary was stopped for one year. After that the Eight Immortals and the Dragon King of the East Sea reconciled. And peace and tranquility were restored to the world.

The story of the Eight Immortals Crossing the Sea has been passed down from generation to generation and has had profound influence on Chinese culture. In Chinese history, literary and artistic works about the Eight Immortals are very popular. In ancient architecture, there are also many carvings and paintings of the Eight Immortals. They were even on sedans taken brides in ancient times. Similarly, there were different patterns and lifelike models of the Eight Immortals. On the blue and white porcelain vases which were popular in the Ming Dynasty, there are designs with the Queen Mother of the West in the center where the scene of the Eight Immortals congratulating her on her birthday could be found. And there is also a special kind of square table known as "the Eight Immortals table." All these works prove the significant influence of the Eight Immortals on people's life. Today, Penglai City in Shandong Province is home to a 5A level national scenic spot——Eight Immortals Crossing the Sea Scenic Spot, where visitors can experience the charm of the mythical legend of Eight Immortals Crossing the Sea. Various films and television series based on the story have been produced and are very popular among the Chinese audience. The impact of the story on the folk culture of China has helped form an intricate system involving many fields such as art, religion, literature, etc. It is undoubtedly a great treasure in Chinese marine legends.

罗刹奇闻寓真知

第九章

Chapter

Nine

The Luo-Cha Country and the Sea-Market

古有大禹，决九川，距四海，遂定九州，是为海内。至此，乃分海之内外。所谓海外，仍有四方，诸国立于烟波浩渺之间，多有异闻流传。于此异闻之中，就有一个关于罗刹国的故事，读来发人深思。

古时，有个叫马骥的人，长相俊美，年少倜傥，喜爱歌舞，十四岁中了秀才，颇有名气。他的父亲是个商人，教他做生意继承家业。一次，马骥出海经商，遭遇风暴，漂到一个从不知晓的城市。马骥上岸进了城，看见市井中的人，长相十分丑陋，而路人见到马骥却纷纷面露惧色而逃。马骥不解，直到穿过城池，来到一个山村，才和几个相貌稍微正常的人搭上了话。马骥这才知道原来这里叫作罗刹国，国中之人以丑为美，他原本长相俊美，在这里却成了怪物。且国中不以才能论人，只依相貌，越丑之人越有高官厚禄；长得最丑的做大官，稍差一点的做小官，再差一点的也能

In ancient times, Yu the Great[1] divided the world according to nine rivers and four seas. The rivers and seas made up what was called Nine Provinces, otherwise known as the "inside sea". The "outside sea" for its part, was composed of different territories. There were many countries stretching over a wide expanse of mist-covered waters from which many stories emanated and were passed down. The following story about Luo-Cha Country was one of the most popular.[2]

Once upon a time, there lived a handsome young man called Ma Ji. Unconventional and unrestrained, he was fond of songs and dances. At fourteen, he passed the imperial examination[3] at the county level and settled down to make a name for himself. However, as the son of a merchant, he took over the business as his father was getting old. One day, when the young man was going on a business trip, his ship was suddenly carried away by a typhoon. After he was tossed around for many days and nights, he finally found himself in a country where everybody was hideously ugly. When the locals saw Ma Ji, they were so terrified that all of them ran away. Ma was very confused. At last he found a village where the inhabitants bore some facial resemblance to ordinary men. Ma finally had the chance to talk to someone and

❶

Yu the Great (2200-2100BC) was a legendary ruler in ancient China famed for his introduction of flood control, inaugurating dynastic rule in China by establishing the Xia Dynasty, and for his upright moral character.

❷

This story is adapted from Strange Stories from a Chinese Studio（《聊斋志异》）, which is a collection of classical Chinese stories by Pu Songling（蒲松龄）. It comprises close to five hundred "marvel tales" in the zhiguai（志怪）and chuanqi（传奇）styles which serve to implicitly criticize societal issues. With the main characters being ghosts, foxes, immortals and demons, the author used the supernatural and the unexplainable to illustrate his ideas of society and government.

❸

Imperial examination was a civil service examination system in Imperial China to select candidates for the state bureaucracy. It became widely utilized as the major path to office in the mid-Tang Dynasty and remained so until its abolition in 1905.

受到贵人的宠爱。马骥听后决定和村人到罗刹国都城去一看究竟。

马骥来到都城后，好奇地四处张望。这时正好下朝，一群人簇拥着一顶大轿子从朝门出来，村人指着说：“这是宰相。”马骥一看，那人两耳后翻，有三个鼻孔，睫毛长如帘子盖住了眼睛。接着后面又出来几个骑马的人，村人挨着指出各人的官职，大都是披头散发、相貌狰狞的丑八怪。官职越低的，丑相也渐减。几日后国中大小官员也听说了马骥的大名想要一见，村人只好把马骥送到了官府去。官员们虽好奇，却都怕得只敢从门缝看去。只有曾出使外国的执戟郎把马骥奉为上宾。那执戟郎眼睛突出，胡须长得像刺猬。他见到马骥十分高兴，告诉他说自己出使过许多国家，唯独没有去过中国。

第二天，执戟郎上朝，把马骥推荐给天子。国王高兴地要下诏书召见，朝中大夫却以马骥样子怪异为由阻止。马骥便住在执戟郎家，二人时常同饮同醉。一天两人喝得正酣，马骥趁着酒兴拔剑起舞,用煤粉抹在脸上扮作张飞表演起来。执戟郎看了认为很美，说：“请你扮成张飞去见宰相，宰相一定乐意用你，高官厚禄不难到手。”马骥答：“只做嬉闹还行，怎么能换个假脸去谋取荣华富贵呢？”执戟郎一再劝

that was when he learned that the country was called Luo-Cha. The countrymen told him that in Luo Cha, everything did not depend on ability, but on appearance. They further told him that people there regarded ugliness as beauty; the uglier you were, the higher your position would be. The extraordinarily ugly were made ministers of state; the less ugly were judges and magistrates; the next in line in terms of looks were employed in the palace of the emperor. In his own country Ma Ji might be a handsome man, but here, he was as ugly as a monster, and that was exactly why the locals were so afraid of him. Hearing about this, Ma was so curious that he decided to go to the capital city with some countrymen.

They arrived just at the end of the morning meeting when all officials were coming out of the court. Pointing at someone, the village people said, "That is the Prime Minister." He was incredibly ugly. He had three nostrils, his ears drooped backward in flaps, and his eye-lashes hung in front of his eyes like bamboo screens. Then several people approached on horseback. The villagers said they were privy councilors. And as they went by, Ma Ji was told the ranks of all the ugly fellows he saw. The lower they got down in hierarchy, the less hideous the officials looked. A few days later, many people heard about Ma and some of the gentry and officials wanted to meet him. However, the officials did not dare to talk to him directly. All they did was to peep at him through their windows. The only person who treated him as a distinguished guest was a man who had been sent to foreign countries on official business by a former king. The man had protruded eye-balls and a beard which was as stiff as the hair of a hedge-hog. He said he was very glad to meet Ma, because he'd been to many countries except

诱，马骥只得应了。执戟郎遂备下酒筵，请达官贵人们前来欢饮，并让马骥涂黑了脸出来相见。客人惊讶地说：“奇怪，先前如此丑陋，今天又这样漂亮！”第二天，大官们纷纷上奏天子，推荐马骥。天子向他询问治国安邦的办法，马骥一一陈述。天子听了赞叹不已，在别宫赐宴款待，并封他为下大夫。时间长了，朝中官员都知道了马骥的面目是假的。他无论走到哪里，总是看见人们小声耳语，不愿意同他接近。马骥感到很孤立，心中不安，就上书要辞去官职。天子不准，只给了他三个月的假期。于是马骥坐着车载着钱财回到了山村，他把金钱分给当时结交的那些朋友，村民们高兴万分，欢声雷动。分到钱的村民告诉马骥他们要去海市，寻求些珍贵玩物，来报答马骥。马骥询问海市的所在，村民告诉他：海市在海底，是四海鲛人卖珠宝的地方，到时四方十二国，都去那里做买卖。马骥听了十分心动，便和村民约定一起去海市。

几天后，马骥和村人将钱物装船，一起朝海市出发。船在海上像飞箭一样行进，走了三天，远远看见水云荡漾之中，群楼重阁，往来商船密集如蚁群。等到城中，集市上摆放的货物，全是奇珍异宝，人世罕有。不多时，一少年骑着骏马走来，集市上的人都急忙躲开，说是东海三太

China.

On the following day, the man recommended Ma Ji to the emperor. The emperor was intrigued, so he ordered that Ma Ji be brought to his palace. Several of the ministers, however, said that Ma's appearance was so hideous that he might frighten Majesty. As a result, the emperor retrieved his order. From then on, Ma Ji stayed at the man's home and they often drank together. One day when they were both drunk, Ma seized a sword, smeared his face with coal dust and began a sword dance. He mimicked Zhang Fei[1], a famous general in China. When the man saw this, he was extremely delighted. He asked Ma Ji to meet the Prime Minister and perform like Zhang Fei. Ma replied, "I don't mind a little amateur acting, but how can I play the hypocrite for my own personal advantage?" However, he consented after the man pressed further. The man prepared a grandiose feast and invited some of the highest officials. Prior to the feast, he instructed Ma Ji to paint himself the way he had previously done. When the guests arrived, Ma was brought out to see them. When they saw him, they all exclaimed, "That's weird! How does it come that he was so ugly before but so handsome now?" By-and-by, when they were all drinking wine, Ma began to chant the most bewitching song. They got so excited that the next day, they recommended him to the emperor. The emperor specifically summoned Ma Ji to come to his palace. When Ma arrived, he asked him many questions about how China was governed. After hearing of Ma's detailed answers the Majesty was full of admiration. Out of delight, the emperor immediately made him a privy councilor. Yet as time went by, his fellow-officials found out the secret about his painted face. So, whenever he was present, they whispered together

[1] Zhang Fei: Zhang Fei was a military general who served under the warlord Liu Bei in the late Eastern Han Dynasty and early Three Kingdoms period of China.

子来了。太子过来，看见马骥，见他相貌不俗，便让仆从询问马骥的籍贯，马骥如实相告。太子很高兴，给了马骥一匹马，邀他同行。

二人出了西城，刚到岸边，马嘶叫着跃进水中，马骥吓得失声喊叫。却见海水从中间分开，两边的水像墙壁一样屹立着。不一会儿，看见一座宫殿。马骥下马，太子拱手将他请入，引荐给端坐殿上的龙王。太子道："儿臣游览海市，遇见这位中华贤士，领他来参见父王。"马骥上前跪拜行礼。龙王说："先生既是饱学之士，定才过屈宋，劳烦写一篇关于海市的文章。"马骥叩头答应，立时写了篇千余字的文章。龙王十分嘉许，接着召集龙族，并在采霞宫举行盛宴将爱女许配给马骥。成亲之后，龙王封马骥为驸马都尉，并把他写的《海市赋》送到四海龙宫传阅。四海龙王纷纷派人前来祝贺，争着下请柬请驸马赴宴。马骥身穿锦绣华服，坐着青龙拉的车子，游遍各处。

在龙宫的时间久了，马骥开始思念家乡。他和龙女商量暂时回家探望一下父母，之后再回来团聚。龙女却说："我们的情缘已经到头了。"马骥非常悲痛。但龙女告诉他自己已怀有身孕，嘱咐马骥虽不再相见，但仍望各自坚守贞洁，不再婚娶，以三年为期，三年后将送还马骥的孩子。话已至

and avoided getting close to him. Consequently, Ma was left to himself and he grew to dislike his position. Because of this, he submitted his resignation, but his request was rejected. He then complained that his health was deteriorating, so he was granted a three-month sick leave. He packed up his valuables and returned to the village. Upon his arrival, the villagers went down on their knees and Ma distributed gold and jewels to all his friends. They were excited to see him. They said, "Your kindness shall be repaid when we go to the sea-market. We will bring you some precious rare gifts." Ma asked them where the sea-market was. They replied that it was located at the bottom of the sea, where mermaids kept their treasure and where as many as twelve countries converged to trade. Ma was interested in learning more about this place, so he decided to go there with the villagers.

Several days later, Ma Ji and the villagers packed up and went on board to the sea-market. Like an arrow, their vessel tore through the water. Three days later, they could see faint outlines of towers and minarets and crowds of trading vessels far off in the distance. When they entered the city, they saw rare pearls and wondrous precious stones of dazzling beauty laid out in the market. After a while, a young man came forward. He was riding a beautiful steed. The people in the market immediately stood back to let him pass. They said he was the third son of the Dragon King of the East Sea. When the prince noticed Ma, he immediately ordered an attendant to ask what his name was and where he was from. Ma bowed and truthfully replied. The prince was very pleased. He offered Ma a horse and invited him to hang out with him.

They went out of the west city gate and down to the sea-shore

此，马骥只好把在罗刹国得到的一对赤玉莲花作为信物交给龙女。天亮后龙女乘白羊车送马骥到海边，道过“珍重”，掉转车头在海水中消失不见。

马骥回到家中，家人非常惊异。马家父母还健在，见儿子回来后十分高兴，便赶着给他张罗婚事。马骥牢记龙女的叮嘱，不再娶妻。三年期限满后，马骥乘船来到约定的岛上，看见两个小孩坐在水面上，拍水嬉闹。仔细看去，两个孩子，一男一女，相貌都很俊秀。额上花冠各点缀着一块玉，便是那赤玉莲花。背上有个锦囊，马骥拆开一看，是龙女所写书信，信中话别离，言情谊，哀而不伤，并特别嘱咐一年后婆婆安葬时，自己将亲临墓穴，尽儿媳孝道。马骥反复读着书信，泪流不止，最后只好抱着孩子掉转船头，满腹惆怅地回去了。

马骥知道母亲的寿命将尽，就提前备好衣服棺木，并在墓地上种植了百余株松树。过了一年，母亲果然去世了。灵柩刚到墓地，就有一个穿孝服的女子走近哭吊。众人正吃惊地看她时，忽然风激雷轰，转眼间那女子就已不见。后来人们又注意到，新种的松树本来大都枯萎了，这时又全活了。马骥的儿子稍长大一点，常常思念母亲，就自己投入大海，几天后才回来。女儿则常常关上门独自哭泣。一次，天空忽

whereupon their horses plunged into the water. Ma was frozen with fright. He screamed out loud. But the sea divided before them and later a wall of water was formed on either side. In no time, they were at the Dragon King's palace. They got off their horses and went in, and Ma was introduced to the king. The young prince said, "Your Majesty, I went to the sea-market, and met this gentleman from China, so I brought him here to meet you." The king said, "A talented scholar like you must be proficient at writing. I'd venture to ask you for a few stanzas about our sea-market." Ma thereupon kowtowed and obeyed the king's command by immediately rolling off several thousand odd verses. The king read them and praised Ma's literary prowess. Then, summoning the members of the royal family, the king held a big feast in the Colored Cloud Palace. Then he betrothed his beloved daughter to Ma who was duly recognized as a royal son-in-law and, by virtue of that, became a state officer. His outstanding poetic talent brought him fame from far and near and the Dragon Kings of the Four Seas sent officers to congratulate him. They competed with each other in their efforts to invite him to their kingdoms. Ma was gorgeously dressed as he went forth riding an azure dragon. He visited every marine kingdom and became a household name everywhere he went.

After a long time in the Dragon Palace, Ma began to miss his homeland. He said to the princess, "I have now been away from my own country for three years. During this time, I have been separated from my father and mother. I'm going to visit my parents and we will soon meet again." But his wife averred, "Our marriage life is coming to an end." Hearing that Ma was very grieved, and tears began to well up in his eyes. The princess continued, "I am pregnant now. So, in spite of

龙女

the separation, I hope we can be faithful to each other in three years. And three years later, when you once more steer your course for this country, I will give you your child." The princess asked for some token of remembrance, and Ma gave her a pair of jade lotuses that he had received during his stay in the Luo-Cha Country. The princess, in a carriage drawn by snow-white sheep, accompanied him to the border of the marine kingdom, where he dismounted and stepped ashore. "Farewell!" cried the princess, as her carriage quickly took her back and as the sea, closing over her, snatched her husband from her sight.

Ma's return shocked his family. His parents were thrilled when he came back. They wanted him to get married without delay but he kept his promise to the princess and refused his parents' suggestion. Then, three years passed and he started across the sea on his return journey. He noticed two children playing in the water. They were riding on the wave-crests and splashing about the water. Upon close examination, Ma saw that they were a boy and a girl. They were both very lovely and wore embroidered caps adorned with jade lotuses. On the back of one of them was a silk bag. In the bag, Ma found a letter from the princess. The letter described their separation, which was mournful but not distressing. The princess also made a promise that the following year, when his mother would pass away, she would visit her grave and perform her duty of filial piety as a daughter-in-law. Ma read the letter over and over again as tears streamed down his cheeks. As he contemplated the immense expanse of the ocean that stretched away to meet the sky, Ma sorrowfully took his children home.

Knowing, too, that his mother would not last long, he prepared everything that was needed for the interment ceremony. He also

然阴云密布，龙女转瞬而至，劝女儿说：“儿已长大，为何哭泣？”说着赐她一棵八尺高的珊瑚树，一帖龙脑香，一百颗明珠，一对八宝嵌金盒子，作为嫁妆。马骥知道龙女来了，急忙跑进来，拉着手就哭。顷刻间，一声疾雷震破房顶，龙女已经不见了。

马骥罗刹国奇遇的故事告一段落，但故事中的情节却让人不由慨叹。马骥原本放浪不羁，至异国他乡却装出一副假面孔来迎合世俗，换取高官厚禄。罗刹国颠倒美丑、曲意逢迎，正是世间丑态的真实写照。马骥虽中秀才，但实际上学问并不精通，然而却在吹捧中自觉比过屈宋，他数日当中名扬四海，不过是如同海市蜃楼一般的虚名。他回乡探望父母，又想与龙女再续情缘，仙凡有别，岂能两全？如此种种，让人警醒。

这样的故事并不只见于中国的海洋文明中，西方也有格列佛流落海外奇国的故事。在小人国，国王挑选官员是以在悬空的绳子上跳舞的技术好坏来决定的。官员们总是随身携带绳子，以便随时取悦国王。许多官员甚至不惜摔断脖子丢掉性命。其荒诞迂腐与罗刹国并无二致。飞岛国的科学家，凶狠愚蠢，一边从事着从黄瓜中提取阳光、把粪便还原为食物这类荒诞不经的科学研究，一边以残暴的

planted over a hundred young pine-trees on the grave. One year later, the old lady died. Her coffin was borne to its last resting-place, and there, was the princess standing by the side of the grave. The on-lookers were surprised. At that moment, there was a flash of lightning which was followed by a clap of thunder and a squall of rain. Then she vanished. Then the people noticed that many of the young pine-trees that had withered were suddenly brought to life. Subsequently, his son went to the sea in search of his mother that he missed so much. After a few days, he finally returned. His daughter wept a lot in secret. One dark day, her mother entered her room and said to the girl, "My child, you have grown up. Why are you still shedding these tears?" Then, as her dowry, she gave her daughter an eight-feet tall coral tree, some dipterocarpus turbinatus[1], one hundred valuable pearls, and two boxes inlaid with gold and precious stones. Having discovered that his wife was around, Ma rushed in and seized her hand as he wept for joy. But suddenly, a violent peal of thunder rent the building and the princess, once again, was gone in a flash.

With this, we come to the end of Ma Ji's adventure in the Luo-Cha Country and the sea-market. The plots of the story are worth reflecting. Ma was an unconventional and unrestrained man, but he disguised himself in a foreign country to ingratiate himself with others in order to obtain a high position and good salary. People in the Luo-Cha Country treated ugliness as beauty and did everything to please the emperor. This appears to be the reflection of the world at its worst. Although Ma had passed the imperial examination, he was, in fact, not

[1] Dipterocarpus turbinatus is a species of tree in the family Dipterocarpus native to north-eastern India and mainland Southeast Asia and cultivated in surrounding areas. In herbal medicine, the plant has been traditionally used for treating gonorrhea, leprosy, psoriasis and other skin diseases. In the home-gardens of South China, it is cultivated both as a medicinal and as a perfume plant.

手段对付民众。人民稍有叛逆，就驾飞岛阻隔阳光，甚至压在居民头上。这些脱离实际、沉溺于幻想的科学家和自觉才华过人博得虚名的马骥又有什么不同呢？

异闻也，多笑谈耳。然世人道：异闻足笑也，此中真知，亦只付笑谈乎？无论是中国，还是西方，在各自的海洋文明中，都有着看似荒诞奇异，实则发人深思的故事。这些海外奇谈反映了人类对自身人性的审视与思考，孕育着文明进步的真知灼见。

proficient in scholarship. But through flattery, his fame spread far and wide just in several days. In addition, Ma wanted to visit his parents and at the same time, maintain the relationship with the princess. Yet common people are different from immortals, so there's no way for human beings to realize all their desires. All in all, there is a lot behind this story for us to think about.

Stories of this nature have not been limited to Chinese marine civilization. In fact, they have also appeared in the west. An example is Gulliver's Travels. In Lilliput, the selection of officials was based on how well they danced on the suspended rope. Officials consistently carried ropes and were always ready to flatter the king. Many officials were even willing to break their necks and die. The degree of absurdity is similar to that of the Luo-Cha Country. The scientists of the flying island are fierce and stupid. They carried out ridiculous experiments to extract sunlight from cucumbers and transform feces into food. If inhabitants showed the slightest sign of rebellion, the scientists used the island to block the sun and even press it on their heads. There is little difference between these unrealistic scientists who indulged in idle fancy and Ma Ji who considered himself brilliant and earned undeserved reputation.

The strange stories seem to be ridiculous and funny. But the problems revealed by these stories cannot be laughed off. There are stories that appear to be superficially bizarre and absurd, but are, in reality, thought-provoking in both Chinese and Western marine civilizations. They reflect human nature and our self-examination about our culture. Through these stories, we have the wonderful experience of gaining insight into ourselves and the society we live in.

海上仙山缥缈见

第十章

Chapter

Ten

Fairy Mountains in the Sea

在中国的古代神话传说中，昆仑山一脉，是西方陆上仙山，而蓬莱则是东方海上仙山。关于二者的传说有很多，第一章中就讲到了归墟中五座仙山的故事。但海上仙山往往难觅踪迹，我们就来说一说这缥缈仙山的传闻。

佛家把世界分为四大部洲：东胜神洲、西牛贺洲、南赡部洲和北俱芦洲。东胜神洲海外有一国土，叫作傲来国。国近大海，海中有一座名山，是为花果山。此山为十洲之祖脉，三岛之来龙，自开清浊而立，鸿蒙判后而成，是座赫赫有名的仙山。花果山势镇汪洋，威宁瑶海，有着丹崖怪石，削壁奇峰。丹崖上，彩凤双鸣，削壁前，麒麟独卧。峰头时听锦鸡鸣，石窟每观龙出入。林中有寿鹿仙狐，树上有灵禽玄鹤。瑶草奇花不谢，青松翠柏长春。仙桃常结果，修竹每留云。一条涧壑藤萝密，四面原堤草色新。正是百川会处擎天柱，万劫无移大地根。

In ancient Chinese mythology, there are numerous legends about Kunlun Mountains and Mount Penglai. Kunlun Mountains are the fairy mountain chains located in Western China, while Mount Penglai is a fairy mountain located in the East Sea. We did mention the five mountains in Guixu in the first chapter of this book and now, we recount stories about fairy mountains which are extremely difficult to be found in the sea.

In Buddhism,the world was divided into the following four continents: Purvavideha, Jambudvipa, Aparagodaniya and Uttarakuru. Beyond Purvavideha, there was a country called Aolai located next to an ocean. In the middle of that ocean was a famous island called Mountain of Flowers and Fruits. The mountain was the ancestral artery of the Ten Continents and the origin of the Three Islands. It was a well-known mountain since earth was first separated from heaven and there were some verses to prove its existence:

It stills the ocean with its might,
It awes the jade sea into calm.
Red cliffs and strange rocks;
Beetling crags and jagged peaks.
Paired phoenixes on red cliffs sing;
Before the beetling crags lone unicorns lie.
The cry of pheasants is heard upon the peaks;
In caves the dragons come and go.

There are deer of long life and magic foxes in the woods;
Miraculous birds and black cranes in the trees.
There are beautiful flowers and strange plants that wither not;

花果山山顶有一块通灵仙石，它吸日月精华，内中孕育了仙胞。一日通灵仙石迸裂，产一石卵，似圆球样大。因见风，化作一个石猴。五官俱备，四肢皆全。便学爬学走，拜了四方。目运两道金光，射冲斗府，惊动天庭。后来，那石猴机缘巧合之中发现山上的一处水帘洞府,遂带领群猴进入，拜为美猴王。花果山上，水帘洞中，美猴王与群猴逍遥数载之后，忧于自己无法长生，终将入地府，就决定外出寻仙拜师。行八九载之后，至西牛贺洲灵台方寸山。山中有座斜月三星洞，洞中有一个神仙，名为菩提祖师，美猴王通过考验，终成菩提祖师座下弟子，并得法号孙悟空。其后数年中，孙悟空悟长生妙道，练七十二般变化，习筋斗云，学成后已是神通了得。后因在同门中过于卖弄，被菩提祖师遣出师门，得归花果山。

回到花果山之后，孙悟空剿了霸占水帘洞的混世魔王，后因凡间兵器不称手，便在猴子猴孙的建议下赴东海龙宫借宝，遂有大闹东海龙宫一说。在龙宫中，孙悟空尽显威风，大捍刀、九股叉、方天画戟通通不要。龙王见宫中虾兵蟹将多有伤损，自己又无可奈何，只得将天河定底的神珍铁说与孙悟空。原以为猴王拿不动神铁，不料神铁认主，恰变为趁手的如意金箍棒。孙悟空乘势索要披挂一副，东海龙王拿不

Green pine and bluish cypress ever in leaf,
Magic peaches always in fruit.
Clouds gather round the tall bamboo.
The wisteria grows thick around the mountain brook
And the banks around are newly-colored with flowers.
It is the Heaven-supporting pillar where all the rivers meet.
The Earth's root, unchanged through a myriad eon.

There was once a magic stone on top of this mountain. Since creation, it had received the might of Heaven, the beauty of Earth, the essence of the Sun and the splendor of the Moon. Due to their influence, it eventually developed miraculous powers including a magic womb. Then one day, the womb burst open and out came a stone egg about the size of a ball. When the wind blew on this egg, it turned into a stone monkey which possessed the five senses and four limbs. When the stone monkey had learned to crawl, then walk, he bowed to all the creation of God. As its eyes moved, two beams of golden light shot towards the Pole Star Palace and startled the supreme heavenly sage, the Jade Emperor of the Azure Vault of Heaven. Then the stone monkey found a cave called Water Curtain Cave on the mountain and leapt into it. The cave had a host of monkeys who all bowed, then lay prostrate and called the stone monkey Handsome Monkey King. In the morning they roamed the Mountain of Flowers and Fruits and in the evening, they settled down for the night in the Water Curtain Cave. They thoroughly enjoyed themselves for years. But the Handsome Monkey King constantly worried about death because he understood the underworld was ruled by the King of Hell. He felt that when the time came for them to die, they would be unable to continue living among the Blessed and this would mean they had lived in vain. To avoid this, they decided to find the

孙悟空

Immortals and Sages who were free from the Wheel of Reincarnation. It took the Handsome Monkey King eight to nine years to arrive at the Spirit Tower Heart Mountain, Jambudvipa. In this mountain was the Cave of the Setting Moon and the Three Stars where an immortal called Patriarch Subhuti lived. After passing the test, the Handsome Monkey King became a disciple of Patriarch Subhuti and was given the name Sun Wukong. Over the years, Sun Wukong learned how to transfigure himself into seventy-two forms and how to ride "somersault cloud". However, as Sun Wukong showed off the skill in front of people, he was punished by the patriarch who ordered him to return to the Water Curtain Cave on the Mountain of Flowers and Fruits.

The Handsome Monkey King returned home in glory. He brought with him a large sword he had captured after killing the Demon King of Confusion. From then on, he practiced military arts every day. Weapons used by mortals were not good enough for him, so his fellow monkeys advised the Handsome Monkey King to ask for a weapon from the Dragon Palace of the East Sea. Hence, there is a story about Sun Wukong causing havoc in the Dragon Palace.

Sun Wukong showed his prowess in the Dragon Palace but didn't take the large sword, the nine-pronged spear or the patterned heavenly halberd. The Dragon King had no choice but to bring out the piece of miraculous iron. The Dragon King had thought that Sun Wukong would be unable to pick it up, but the miraculous iron transformed into a Golden Cudgel. Upon Sun Wukong's approach, the cudgel glowed to signify it had found its true master. It could also change its size and, depending on his master's whim, multiply and fight. At the same time, Sun Wukong asked the Dragon King to give him an armor. The Dragon King said he

出，就擂鼓敲钟召来其他三海龙王。三个龙王唯唯诺诺献上锁子黄金甲，凤翅紫金冠和藕丝步云履。孙悟空穿戴一新，正是个威风凛凛的美猴王。至于大闹天宫，被压在五指山下，保唐僧取经，历九九八十一难，都是后话。唯称猴王、修仙法、得如意金箍棒是这仙山上饶有趣味的故事。

傲来国花果山，是佛家所说十洲之祖脉，三岛之来龙，无疑是海上仙山之首。而道家也有十洲三岛之说，虽佛道两家所说是否一致还有待考证，但此中诸多异闻仍值得一讲。如此，我们就讲一讲十洲中的聚窟洲。

所谓十洲，乃是祖洲、瀛洲、玄洲、炎洲、长洲、元洲、流洲、生洲、凤麟洲、聚窟洲。据《十洲记》记载，汉武帝征和三年，月支国国王派遣使者进贡了一枚大如雀卵、黑如桑椹的返魂香。使者对汉武帝解释此香来之不易，说道:“(臣国)搜奇蕴而贡神香，步天林而请猛兽，乘毳车而济弱渊，策骥足以度飞沙。契阔途遥，辛苦蹊路。用了十三年才搜罗到此灵物，并进献给上国。”但汉武帝不认得此物，就以非中国所有为由而交付外库。除了返魂香，使者还献上仙山之中的异兽，这灵兽形如五六十日大的幼犬，狐狸般大小，皮毛为黄色。虽然体型小，使者却称它为猛兽。猛兽一叫，如天大雷霹雳，两目光朗冲天。同时，人则颠蹶伏地，牛马猪

had none. So he was left with no option but to strike the bell and beat the drums to solicit help from his brothers. The three Dragon Kings brought out a pair of lotus-root cloud-walking shoes, a suit of golden chain mail and a phoenix-winged purple gold helmet. Sun Wukong put on the golden helmet and the armor as well as the cloud-walking shoes, then charged out waving his cudgel. There are stories about the havoc that ensued the one in the Dragon Palace, how Sun Wukong was eventually imprisoned under the Five-Finger Mountain by Buddha and how he accompanied Monk Tang Sanzang on a journey to retrieve Buddhist sutras from the West - a test of endurance during which he encountered eighty-one tribulations. But they all happened later. Only the stories about having the name Handsome Monkey King, how to achieve immortality and how to obtain the Golden Cudgel were linked to the fairy mountains because they happened there.

The Mountain of Flowers and Fruits in Aolai country is the ancestral heartbeat of the Ten Continents and the origin of the Three Islands among Buddhists. It is undoubtedly the head of the fairy mountains. It is also necessary to note that Ten Continents and Three Islands are also mentioned in Taoism. Although the consistency of the two versions among Buddhists and Taoists remains to be verified, many existing anecdotes are worth mentioning. Here, we will talk about Juku, one of the Ten Continents.

The Ten Continents include Zu Continent, Ying Continent, Xuan Continent, Yan Continent, Chang Continent, Yuan Continent, Liu Continent, Sheng Continent, Fenglin Continent and Juku Continent. In 90 BC, the king of Yuezhi country sent an envoy to tribute the soul-recalling incense to the then Emperor Wu of Han Dynasty (156–87BC). The incense was as big as a birds egg and as black as a mulberry. The

envoy told the emperor that the soul-recalling incense was hard-earned. He said, "We have collected many rare treasures and just picked out the soul-recalling incense for Your Majesty. And we went deep into the wooded hills to find beasts, sat on the sleighs into the dark abyss and rode horses through the desert. It was a long and hard journey. And it took us 13 years to find this treasure and present it to Your Majesty." But Emperor Wu of Han didn't recognize the value of this treasure. As a result, he consigned it to the warehouse outside the palace. Besides, the envoy also sent a fabulous fox-sized, yellow-fur beast that was shaped like a fifty or sixty-day old puppy. Although it was small, the messenger called it a beast of prey. Whenever the beast roared, it sounded like a crash of thunder. Two beams of golden light shot towards the sky when its eyes moved. At the same time, people fell to the ground, and animals such as cattle, horses, pigs and dogs were frightened and sought for cover. Seeing this strange animal, the tiger was so afraid that it just lay on the ground motionlessly as if it were dead. The beast climbed on the tiger's head and urinated into the tiger's mouth. The tiger did not dare to move. The next day, when the Emperor wanted to accept the beast, both the envoy and the beast disappeared. They looked for them but found nothing.

In the first year of Houyuan[1], there was an epidemic in the capital city Chang'an (present-day Xi'an, Shaanxi Province) which killed more than half of the people. Then the Emperor Wu of Han Dynasty remembered the soul-recalling incense which the envoy had gave him as

[1] Houyuan (后元) is the 11th and also the last Chinese era name (年号) of the Emperor Wu of Han. A Chinese era name is the regnal year, reign period, or regnal title used as a traditional way to number years in an emperor' sreign and name certain Chinese rulers. Some emperors have several era names, one after another, where each beginning of a new era resets the numbering of the year back to year one or yuan (元). The numbering of the year increases on the first day of the Chinese calendar each year.

狗之等，惊吓万分，很久才恢复。上林苑中的老虎见到这异兽，伏地不起，恐惧如死虎。异兽径直登上虎头，溺虎口，虎仍不敢动。第二天汉武帝想要收下异兽时，使者与异兽却都消失不见，四处找寻，也毫无消息。

后元元年，长安城内有数百人患病，病死者过半。汉武帝这时想起使者所献返魂香，就命人取出在城内点燃。此时，死了不到三个月的人通通复活。香的气味在城中历时三月仍不散，汉武帝这才相信返魂香是仙山上的神物。再说返魂香燃过之后，虽未增减，且妥善保存，但香味已经消失了。汉武帝既感叹又悔恨，只怪当时没有给使者应有礼遇，问得仙山所在。第二年汉武帝在五柞宫驾崩，只可惜返魂香已失效，再不能使汉武帝复活。因此，有人说这正是汉武帝咎由自取，命数如此。

说罢海内十洲，自然还要说起海上三仙山。《史记·封禅书》有载：蓬莱、方丈、瀛洲。此三神山者。在渤海中，盖尝有至者，诸仙人及不死药在焉。传言三仙山上的神仙有长生不老药，因此历代帝王都视三仙山为长生不老的象征，并多派方士访寻。

在齐威王、齐宣王、燕昭王时代，传言就有人曾到过仙山之上，说神仙与长生不老药都在上面。后来，最有名的寻

tribute, so he ordered that the incense be lit up. As the fragrance traveled, those who had died within the previous three months were all brought back to life. And for three months, the entire city was covered in the fragrance. It was then that the Emperor started to believe that the incense was really something magical from the fairy mountain. However, even though it was well preserved, and no one tampered with it, the fragrance of the incense faded away. The Emperor was very regretful that he had not treated the envoy courteously and respectfully nor asked where the fairy mountain was. The next year, the Emperor passed away at Wuzha Palace. It was such a pity that the soul-recalling incense had lost its effect and could no longer revive the emperor! But some believed it was the Emperor himself who brought this upon his life.

After the islands, we shall then talk about the three fairy mountains. The ancient Chinese book, *Records of the Grand Historian*[1] recounts that "Penglai, Fangzhang and Yingzhou, the three fairy mountains, are located in the Bohai Sea. Someone who once went there claimed it was the place to find immortals and elixir." It was said that the immortals had elixir, therefore emperors of different dynasties sent alchemists to look for the fairy mountains which were regarded as a symbol of long life.

Early in the Warring States Period (475–221BC), it was said that someone had gone to the fairy mountains and that both immortals and elixir were found there. Thereafter, the most famous person to go in search for the fairy mountains was Xu Fu. In Chinese history, Ying Zheng was

[1] *The Records of the Grand Historian*, also known by its Chinese name Shiji (《史记》), is a monumental history of ancient China and the world finished around 94 BC by the Han dynasty official Sima Qian (司马迁). The work covers the world as it was then known to the Chinese and a 2500-year period from the age of the legendary Yellow Emperor (黄帝) to the reign of Emperor Wu of Han (汉武帝) in the author' s own time. It has been called a "foundational text in Chinese civilization" and set the model for the 24 subsequent dynastic histories of China.

访，就是徐福东渡。秦嬴政以武力统一六国，做上了始皇帝，随之生活日渐奢侈，大兴土木，广立碑传，但这挡不住他的日渐衰老。因此，秦始皇愈发想要长生不老。国中方士徐福提请斋戒，与童男女求访仙山，以满足秦始皇长生不老的愿望。但徐福第一次入海求神药，耗时数年，花费甚多，却一无所获。徐福归来后，恐秦始皇降罪，就谎称蓬莱仙山的灵药确实存在，但行程为大蛟鱼所阻，无法到达，药也无法拿到。不久，秦始皇梦到与人状海神相战。占梦之后，便命令入海者携带捕巨鱼的用具，并配备连弩再次出海。但从琅琊北到荣成山，都没有见到巨鱼。到了芝罘，才见到巨鱼，并射杀了一条。后来，秦始皇再次派徐福东渡，并让他带上数千童男女、各种匠人和五谷良种，以显虔诚。但此次出海之后，徐福再也没有回来。秦始皇没有得到长生不老药，最终驾崩于沙丘平台。一众仙人和长生不老药也就仍然隐藏在虚无缥缈的大海之上。

从古至今，许多饱学之士力图通过考据将传说中的仙山与现实中的海岛山川一一对应，虽然会有谬误的存在，但这无疑说明了人们对海上仙山有着极大的兴趣，正是身不能至，神向往之。而在西方海洋神话传说中，和中国仙山类似的传闻并不多，一方面是中国佛道儒并存，除了正

a military dictator who succeeded to be the emperor of China during the Qin Dynasty (221-207BC)——the first dynasty of China. However, as time went by, the emperor became attracted to a luxurious lifestyle. He went in for large-scale constructions and tablet inscriptions. However, all these could not prevent him from aging. Therefore, he increasingly wanted to live forever. At that time, there was an alchemist named Xu Fu who wanted to help the emperor to become immortal. So, he offered, with the company of some boys and girls, to locate the fairy mountains. Several years later, Xu got nothing back after spending a considerable sum of money. In order to avoid punishment, Xu lied to the emperor. He said the magical medicine actually existed in Mount Penglai but they were unable to get it because a giant fish had obstructed them.

Before long, the emperor dreamed about engaging in a fight with a human-like sea god. After the dream, some seafarers were ordered to go out to the sea once more but this time, they carried tools for catching giant fish. They were also armed with continuous-launching crossbows. However, from the north of Langya (an ancient place name, present-day southeastern Shandong Province) to Rongcheng Mountain, no giant fish was seen. Later in Zhifu Island, the seafarers saw giant fishes and shot one. Later, the emperor sent Xu Fu to go to the East again. He sent him out together with thousands of boys and girls, all kinds of craftsmen and grains to show their piety. But after going out to sea, Xu never returned. The emperor failed to get the medicine that would enable him to live forever, so he eventually died at Sand Dunes Palace Platform. Still, the immortals and magical medicine were all hidden in the distant and legendary sea.

Since ancient times, many scholars have tried, using textual research,

仙之外，散仙众多，修行之所遍布各地，因而海上仙山传闻就多了起来。另一方面，西方神话中海神往往居于奥林匹斯山或海底宫殿，并不会住在海岛之上，海上仙山的传闻自然也就没有了出处。因此，可以说，中国海上仙山的传闻是世界海洋文明中的瑰宝。

除了考据，海上仙山的传闻在实际生活中也有着巨大影响。中国的花果山风景区就有十数处之多，蓬莱则有三仙山景区。以海上仙山传闻为架构写就的文学作品更难以数计。看罢今天，再回首过去，古时帝王追求长生，多寻访海上仙山，最终却敌不过历史的潮流，化为东逝水。天地悠悠之间，仙人仙山大概是可遇而不可求，这正是：忽闻海上有仙山，山在虚无缥缈间。

to match the legendary fairy mountains with the real islands and mountains. Though they have not succeeded, their endeavors underscore the great interest people continue to have on fairy mountains in the sea. The expression "I can't get it, but my heart is longing for it" aptly summarizes this phenomenon. In western mythology, there are very few similar legends which are related to fairy mountains. On the one hand, China is a place where Buddhism, Taoism and Confucianism coexist whereas the West is not. In fact, besides orthodox immortals, there is a constellation of immortals with various origins who have helped spread fairytales widely. On the other hand, in western mythology, sea gods often reside on Mount Olympus or undersea palaces, but not on islands. So, legends of the fairy mountains naturally are not popular. Therefore, it can be said that the legends of the Chinese fairy mountains are a treasure of the world's marine civilization.

Apart from facilitating textual research, the legends of fairy mountains in the sea also have a great impact on real life. There are more than a dozen Mountain of Flowers and Fruits scenic spots in China including the Three Fairy Mountains Scenic Area in Penglai. The number of literary works based on the legends of fairy mountains in the sea have continued to increase. Looking back on history, we can find that in order to live forever, many ancient emperors instructed that the fairy mountains must be located. However, none of them succeeded in finding them and eventually they all turned to ashes. Between heaven and earth, the immortals and fairy mountains are probably the most mysterious and unreachable. This exactly proves the lines of the famous Chinese poem The Everlasting Regret:

He learned that on the sea were fairy mountains proud
That now appeared, now disappeared amid the cloud.

参考书目

[加]A. 曼古埃尔、[意]G. 盖德鲁培著，赵蓉译：《想象地名私人词典》，华东师范大学出版社，2016 年。

〔唐〕白居易著，许渊冲译：《画说长恨歌（汉英对照版）》，中译出版社，2017 年。

毕国鹏：《临淄区非物质文化遗产名录》，齐鲁书社，2010 年。

陈益源：《府城大观音亭与观音信仰研究》，里仁书局，2015 年。

当增扎西：《藏族观音文化研究》，中国藏学出版社，2013 年。

党芳莉：《八仙信仰与文学研究——文化传播的视角》，黑龙江人民出版社，2006 年。

〔西汉〕东方朔：《神异经》，上海古籍出版社，1995 年。

董志文：《话说中国海洋神话与传说》，广东经济出版社，2014 年。

窦应泰：《观音全传》，时代文艺出版社，1994 年。

〔唐〕段成式：《酉阳杂俎》，上海古籍出版社，2012 年。

〔南朝宋〕范晔：《后汉书》，中华书局，2007 年。

〔清〕冯梦龙：《情史》，凤凰出版社，2011 年。

符震:《黎族民间故事集》，花城出版社，1982年。

〔东晋〕干宝:《搜神记》，中华书局，2012年。

[英]格里·麦克考尔著，茶健译:《龙—神话传说中的生物》，湖北少儿出版社，2010年。

国家海洋局办公室:《妈祖文化与海洋精神》，海洋出版社，2017年。

胡照华:《中华神龙》，中国城市出版社，2003年。

吉成名:《中国崇龙习俗》，黑龙江教育出版社，2012年。

吉峰:《闽台妈祖文化传播研究》，厦门大学出版社，2017年。

[英]杰拉尔丁·平奇著，邢颖译,《走近埃及神话》，外语教学与研究出版社，2007年。

〔北宋〕李昉:《太平广记》，中华书局，1961年。

〔北宋〕李昉:《太平御览》，中华书局，1960年。

〔北魏〕郦道元:《水经注》，中华书局，2016年。

〔战国〕列子:《列子·汤问篇》，中华书局出版社，2016年。

刘秋霖:《观音——图像与传说》，中国文联出版社，2005年。

〔西汉〕刘向:《列仙传》，学苑出版社，1998 年。

刘志雄、杨静荣:《龙与中国文化》，人民出版社，1992 年。

鲁迅:《中国小说史略 · 明之神魔小说》，中国书籍出版社，2016 年。

鲁谆:《龙文化与民族精神》，上海人民出版社，2007 年。

〔清〕曼陀罗室主人:《观音菩萨的故事》，陕西师范大学出版社，2007 年。

[爱尔兰]帕德里克 · 科勒姆著，邢小胖译:《奥丁的子女:北欧神话故事集》，上海社会科学院出版社，2016 年。

庞进:《八千年中国龙文化》，人民日报出版社，1993 年。

彭文宇:《妈祖文化研究丛论》，人民出版社，2012 年。

〔清〕蒲松龄:《聊斋志异》，中华书局，2009 年。

朴趾源:《热河日记》，上海书店出版社，1997 年。

[英]乔纳森 · 斯威夫特著，杨昊成译:《格列佛游记》，译林出版社，2016 年。

秦贝臻:《护航天使:妈祖信仰与妈祖文化》，北方妇女儿童出版社，2015 年。

〔明〕任昉（南朝梁）：《述异记》，吉林大学出版社，1992 年。

[美]萨缪尔·诺亚·克拉莫尔著，叶舒宪、金立江译：《苏美尔神话》，陕西师范大学出版总社，2013 年。

[英]莎士比亚著，梁宗岱译：《莎士比亚十四行诗》，华东师范大学出版社，2016 年。

〔清〕沈起凤：《谐铎》，岳麓书社，1986 年。

沈瑜庆：《福建通志》，方志出版社，2016 年。

〔明〕司马迁（西汉）：《史记》，中华书局，2009 年。

[德]斯威布著，楚图南译：《希腊神话和传说》，人民文学出版社，2003 年。

孙昌武：《中国文学中的维摩与观音》，天津教育出版社，2005 年。

陶思炎：《中国鱼文化》，中国华侨出版公司，1990 年。

〔清〕陶珽：《说郛三种·徂异记》，上海古籍出版社，2012 年。

〔元〕脱脱：《宋史·卷四》，中华书局，1983 年。

王国良:《海内十洲记研究》，文史哲出版社，1993 年。

王汉民:《八仙与中国文化》，中国社会科学出版社，2000 年。

〔东晋〕王嘉:《拾遗记》，中华书局，1981 年。

〔清〕王椷:《秋灯丛话》，黄河出版社，1990 年。

〔明〕吴承恩:《西游记》，中央编译出版社，2015 年。

〔明〕吴元泰:《四游记》，华夏出版社，2015 年。

邢莉:《观音——神圣与世俗》，学苑出版社，2001 年。

〔明〕许仲琳:《封神演义》，人民文学出版社，2007 年。

[美]依迪丝·汉密尔顿著，刘一南、陈嘉映译:《神话》，华夏出版社，2014。

袁珂:《山海经校注》，北京联合出版社，2014 年。

袁珂:《中国神话传说》，北京联合出版社，2016 年。

袁珂:《中国神话大词典》，华夏出版社，2015 年。

袁珂:《中国神话史》，北京联合出版社，2015 年

袁坷:《中国神话传说词典》，北京联合出版公司，2014 年。

张国栋、柯力:《妈祖文化与当代社会》，厦门大学出版社，

2016年。

〔西晋〕张华:《博物志·卷二·异人》,北京联合出版社,2017年。

〔宋〕张君方:《云笈七签》,中央编译出版社,2016年。

郑丽航、蒋维锬:《妈祖文献史料汇编(第一辑)·档案卷》,中国档案出版社,2011年。

中国民间文学集成全国编辑委员会:《中国民间故事集成·福建卷》,中国ISBN中心,1998年。

中国民间文学集成全国编辑委员会:《中国民间故事集成·浙江卷》,中国ISBN中心,1998年。

钟敬文、刘魁立:《中国民间故事集成·江苏卷》,中国ISBN中心,1998年。

舟欲行、曲实强:《涛声神曲:海洋神话与海洋传说》,海潮出版社,2012年。

〔战国〕庄子:《庄子·大宗师》,中华书局,2016年。

〔战国〕左丘明:《国语》,上海古籍出版社,2015年。

Birrell, Anne, *The Classic of Mountains and Seas*, London: Penguin, Penguin Classics, 1999.

Giles, Herbert A., *Strange Stories from a Chinese Studio*, London: T. De La Rue, 1880.

Mair, Victor H., ed., *The Columbia Anthology of Traditional Chinese Literature*, New York: Columbia University Press, 1994.

Minford, John and Joseph S.M., Lau eds., *Classical Chinese Literature: An Anthology of Translations, Volume I: From Antiquity to the Tang Dynasty*, New York: Columbia University Press & Hong Kong: The Chinese University Press, 2000.

Ouyang Jingyi, *Ba Xian Chuan Qi(Dramas/ Legends of the Eight Immortals)*, Taibei: Ke Shu Bookstore, 1990.

Raban, Johnathan, *The Oxford Book of the Sea*, New York: Oxford University Press, 1993.

Strassberg, Richard, *A Chinese Bestiary: Strange Creatures from the Guideways Through Mountains and Seas*, University of California Press, 2002.

Wang Rongpei, Xiong Zhiqi, *The Complete Works of Tao Yuanming*, Hunan People Publishing House, 2003.

Yu, Anthony C., *The Journey to the West*, University Of Chicago Press, 2012.